New York Showdown

Perry Zyms

New York Showdown

Copyright 2009
Wollaston Press

ISBN 0-9657005-8-5

Wollaston Press
PO Box 862011
Marietta, GA 30062

Type: Times New Roman

Those who cannot remember the past are condemned to repeat it.

George Santayana - 1896

What seems inconceivable today becomes tomorrow's historical fact.

Harry Mills - 2009

For Phyllis
1936 - 2007

❶

Why the hell these kind of things had to happen on Fridays, was something Harry Mills would never understand.   He'd had a stable, if not illustrious career of twenty years on the Police force, risen to the highest level of his ability and then retired into a position as Security Chief for the Midtown Expo Center.   Harry's pension got deposited to his account each month like clockwork.   Of course, he got to see precious little of it after Mrs. Harry got done paying the bills that Harry never wanted to see. Not to worry.   His paychecks from the Expo Center were more than sufficient to keep them going in reasonable style, and the little "tips" he received on occasion from grateful promoters and exhibitors went into Harry's "play" fund which he kept in a safe deposit vault right at the Center.

So here he was at 3 o'clock on a Friday when he was getting ready to head for the shore with his fishing gear and a couple of six packs, when some Goddamn nut faxes a message to say that he's going to take down the Electronika Internationale exhibition set to open next week. Shit!   In all the years that the Center had operated, the worst they had encountered was loading dock thefts and the usual dips who jostled the crowds looking for wallets, cash and credit cards.   Now Harry had a genuine nutter on his hands and he couldn't pretend he had no warning.   The damn fax had come in on the line to the General Manager's office.   It wasn't bad enough that two days earlier everybody was sitting glued to their TVs watching CNN, MSNBC and the other networks as we dealt with the job of urban renewal in Baghdad.

The receptionist in the G.M's inner sanctum, a woman by the name of Tabatha had two problems in life. She couldn't keep either her legs or her mouth shut. By now, everybody including the sweepers probably knew there was a threat to blow up the show. Double shit! 1,200 exhibitors would start moving into the cavernous halls in five days, and in eight days the halls could be crowded with more than 100,000 attendees. It was hard enough in this environment to keep these shows going, without adding another fear factor.

Electronika was the largest show in the world for the gurus, whiz kids and wannabes of the new age. It was touted by the government to foreign buyers, it attracted every major player in the industry from around the world and was easily the area's biggest trade show.

Harry made some mental notes. He had no idea who sent the fax. No idea of what type of device he had to find. No idea of where it could be located, or when it was set to go off. There were only three things he could take for certain. It had to go off on one of the public attendance days when the most people were in the facility. Whoever sent the fax had to be taken seriously. And, if he didn't prevent this bullshit, he was out of a cushy job and looking at an old age of working pick-up shifts at a shopping center in Jersey or checking baggage at the Airport. Harry had to do something. What that something was, he hadn't a clue. His only note on the yellow pad in front of him said, "Call Tom, cancel trip." The weekend Fishing and Beer Swilling Association meetings would have to be called off for the duration.

The minutes seemed to fall off the clock while

Harry's brain feverishly raced to find some starting point that would seem like a cogent plan to deal with this impending disaster. It was only a matter of time before the walkie talkie on his desk would announce a "Code 44 Station 5." In plain language that meant to report personally to Carlton Bentwood, the General Manager at his office and immediately. It was the type of summons any sensible person would want to avoid, and even more so on a nervous Friday afternoon fifteen minutes before quitting time. What the hell to do about this latest load of unwelcome shit? Maybe it was a crank who sent the fax. Maybe it was a nut case. Could even be one of those computer geeks from CCNY.

The odds were that the fax was a hoax. But, there's always that one chance in a thousand that it's for real. It's a chance Harry could take for himself, perhaps. But he couldn't assume that responsibility for 100,000 other people. His pal, Lyle Cudgins, had been chief of security at the embassy in Beirut when the car loaded with bombs had careened into the barricade. Lyle had been warned to watch for exactly that type of attack and had relaxed his vigilance. Boom. A good chunk of the embassy was blown away and there wasn't enough of Lyle left to fill a baggie. Got to take radicals and psychos seriously if you want to stay alive. And since 9-11, the world had changed, even if Harry wished it otherwise.

Harry thought about the throngs that would be pouring in the dozens of entrances of the Expo Center next week. He had exactly 32 people on his staff for this event, most of whom were $12 per hour part timers, who were not exactly super intellects. Throw in another dozen or so that the show promoters would hire to provide crowd control at registration, and they still were not exactly a deterrent force to be reckoned with.

Tom was going to be disappointed that their weekend fishing trip had to be canceled. But, Tom was an old friend who understood that Harry had a mess of somewhat strange people and circumstances to deal with. Anyhow, this would give Tom a golden opportunity to lie about the fish he caught when there were no witnesses. Harry's thoughts were a jumble of rapid fire impressions like you would see in a frenetic TV commercial. POW - there was Mary Mills, his wife of 36 years, feigning happiness that Harry would be at home instead of getting plastered in the name of good clean outdoors fun.

Mary would have a million questions, most of which Harry knew he couldn't answer. Sure, he would fill her in on the threat. But he'd have to downplay the seriousness of the situation to avoid showing his hand, which at this time was a complete bust. No sense in getting Mary too worried. Harry was worried enough for them both. POW - there was Carlton Bentwood, III, his serene highness, the General Manager, or "Carly" as he was known behind his back to Harry and some of the others on the staff. Carly was going to want to know everything and would undoubtedly wind up any briefing with some mealy mouthed line like, "I've got complete confidence in you, Harry. Go get 'em." Christ, he'd heard that same line when the Expo Center was besieged by civil rights marchers, when the sprinkler systems all let go one day during the D. A. R. Convention, and a hundred other times, including when Carlton IV got busted for possession during his junior year at Cornell.

8

Harry smiled.   He had pulled in a marker from a local Sheriff's Deputy to get the punk off.   The evidence had disappeared without explanation.   Young Carly IV was duly graduated, married off to a vacuous blond from Buffalo whose family owned a tractor dealership, and after the honeymoon in Hawaii, Carly-4 had exhibited great ability as ace tractor sales manager, party giver, philanderer and psalm singer.   A chip off the old block.

POW - there was the image of the damn Center going up in a fire ball as a car load of fertilizer gets energized by a couple of drums of kerosene.   Thanks to the guys who brought down the Murrah Federal Building in Oklahoma City, every cretin who knew which end of a shovel to hold could fashion a bomb.   And there was no doubt that the religious zealots would now go after some "soft targets" such as department stores, hotels and trade shows.   The brighter ones could learn via the internet or at their public library.   Although Harry had no idea of just how you did it, he knew that those who were motivated could do it, and the frigging things would work.   It is no comfort to somebody who gets killed or injured to know that the bomb was crude.   A bomb is a bomb, and Harry didn't need one on his watch.

POW - it was not another image on the inside of his closed eyelids.   It was the ringing of his phone.   He grabbed for it.   "Security; . . . Captain Mills."   Too late. The placid tones of HSH Carly-3 wafted through the receiver.   "Harry, this is Carlton.   We seem to have a problem which I believe you have received notice of by means of a fax sent to my office.   Can you come up here for a briefing on the matter?   Say, in five minutes?" Without waiting for any reply, HSH continued, "Good, see

9

you then." and the line went dead.   It was, as usual, a command performance.

Slowly, Harry's 230 pound frame pushed back the swivel chair whose vinyl had long since given up from the daily assault of Harry's use, and he rose to his full 5 foot 10 inch height.   Harry's belt had found a way to accommodate the result of his fishing trips.   His pants were worn to a place somewhat below where his waist would have been, if he still had one.   The angle of declension was about 20 degrees from back to front.   His plain dark blue tie was tacked to his shirt with little golden colored handcuffs and hung a bit short of the belt line and a little south of the neckline.   Harry fastened his collar button, pulled up his tie, wiped each shoe tip on the back of the opposite leg of his trousers and grabbed his hat and walkie as he slammed the door shut behind him on the way to his inquisition.

From the Security Office, which was adjacent to the loading docks, to the Executive Suite was about a five minute walk.   Then up three stories to the Eagles Nest of Carly-3.   There were no exhibitions at the Center this week, so escalators weren't running.   Harry used his key to call the elevator and rode up to meet his boss.

Funny thing about Carly and Harry. They were born within three weeks of each other, but about 6 miles apart.   That six miles might as well have been 6,000 miles, that's how different their worlds had been.   While Harry was going to school in a formerly genteel neighborhood in Queens, Carly was being prepped at a school in Connecticut.   Harry went on to a State College while Carly followed the family tradition by heading off to

Yale. Carly joined a frat. He became a Deke. Harry didn't join a frat. He became a lush.

Carly's family included an ex-mayor, an ex-Senator, two judges, 5 attorneys, and one very influential bank president. Harry's clan counted 3 cops, 1 fire fighter, 11 civil servants and 2 felons. Since Harry knew that the relatives who were working for the city or state were usually neither civil nor doing much service, he felt secure that he was undeniably the senior member of the Mills clan and the voice of authority and success. After all, he had done his time on the cops, got his pension, landed the job with the Center, and was a source of many freebies to all sorts of public and private entertainments. Harry was, in fact, the majordomo of the clan Mills.

Carly had come to his exalted position after a mediocre career in banking. When the bank was forced to write off more than three hundred and twenty million in questionable loans which Carly had authorized to aging fellow Dekes, his career path was detoured by his cousin, Warren. Warren's bank had been the lead underwriter of the financing for the Expo Center and they owed him. Over lunch in Warren's private dining room, it was agreed that the interest rate on the permanent financing might be made considerably less. The next day, Carly's appointment as General Manager was announced in the press.

Harry glanced at his watch as he entered the Executive Inner Temple. It was 4:50 and Tabatha had already left for the day. He strode past the reception area and the glass walled conference room to the walnut double doors which guarded the office of Carlton Bentwood III, as General Manager of the Midtown Expo Center. He knocked twice quickly, opened the door and entered. About forty feet away from the door, Carly-3 was seated behind his immaculate desk. It seemed to Harry the desk was about the size of Rhode Island. The surface of Carly's desk was never disturbed by any papers or other signs of work. Carly prided himself on his organizational skills and ability to delegate. In fact, thought Harry, he had delegated just about everything other than his pay check and the keys to the G.M.'s private bathroom.

Harry approached the desk. Carly seemed not to notice him as he was speaking on the telephone which was installed on the credenza behind him. His conversation completed, Carly turned and smiled. "Hello, Harry. Quite a problem you've got, isn't it." Carly had such a disingenuous way of phrasing things.

"I dunno; could be another squirrel case, Carlton."

"I rather think not, Harry." Carly picked up a fax from his credenza, extended it to Harry and continued, "This came in just about 15 minutes ago. Look at it. The bastard has addressed it to ME! He knows your name, mine and where we live. You have to do something, Harry." It was poignant. *You* had to do something. Not *we*. Harry took the fax in his hands and as he read it his blood started to chill. "Dear Mr Bentwood. Please do not dismiss my prior facsimile message as being the work of a mentally disturbed person. I have spent a good deal of time making my investigation of your facilities, your personnel and even your personal lives. Your wife, Eileen, two kids and your dog, Chipper, all live in a lovely Georgian Colonial in the Hamptons. The assessment on

12

your home was reduced this year to only $2,670,000. I think you probably got a very good deal, since the house is magnificent. Tell Mills that I have spoken with Mary, and driven by the Euston Street house. I didn't pull the assessment figures on Harry's place. My guess would be that it wouldn't sell for more than $460k. You really might think of paying him more; especially if he can prevent my attack on Electronika. As they say in show business, 'break a leg.' We'll be communicating again. I forgot something. You and Harry will have to figure this out for yourselves. If you bring in the Keystone Cops, you up the ante. Sincerely, Sam."

"And you want me to think this guy is for real? This is the work of some certifiable asshole, Carly."

"That may be so, Harry. It may also be the work of some insane son of a bitch who has nothing better to do than blow our asses to Kingdom Come. And, you get paid to make sure these guys don't do things like this. Shit, Harry; Eileen and I are supposed to be in Las Vegas next week. I don't want to have to cancel that trip.

Whadda you think?"

He chose his words carefully and enunciated with equal care. "What I think, Mr. Bentwood, is that you had better cancel that trip. There are people who will need to be called in, and steps which need to be taken which will require your authority and position. If the Center is still standing in two weeks, Las Vegas will still be there."

You could freeze meat in the coldness of Carly's stare. "That serious?"

13

"Yeah. That serious." was the answer.

"Well you get going on this Harry. I'm putting all assets and personnel at your disposal. I know you can handle this one. See me to approve any overtime cards. Otherwise, go get 'em. Honcho."

How nice to know that he was now "Honcho." Chief of everything if things went wrong. Deputy of the Great Man if all came out right. Without another word, the newly commissioned honcho turned and let himself out of the massive office.

Samantha Harrison wasn't a particularly pretty woman.   She stood 5'3" and weighed a bit more than she ought to for that height.   She wasn't fat, nor was she slim. Every day Samantha would pass by hundreds of people on the streets of New York, and none of them would be turning to stare after her.   Her auburn hair was cut medium length and hung fairly straight about her otherwise plain face.   She dressed conservatively in the style of masses of office workers.   Samantha wore low heels, and she often wore simple dresses with modest V-necklines. Around her neck was a simple necklace of little gold balls. She wore a small amethyst ring on her right hand, a $15 watch from a pushcart vendor on her left wrist, and plain hoop earrings.   Samantha's figure was obviously female, but hardly voluptuous.   She was truly homely in the sense of that word as meaning plain and unpretentious.   To Samantha, that very plainness was a protective coloration allowing her to pass unnoticed and unmolested through life.

Her growing up years were marked by a series of economic upheavals.   Her father was one of those people who cursed the dawning of the information age which had ejected him from one paper shuffling job after another.   By the time Samantha was eleven years old,   Paul Harrison had abandoned all pretense of trying to find work. He couldn't embrace the computer chip, and turned instead to the bottle.   As his self esteem and financial fortunes sank ever lower, he became abusive of Samantha and her mother.   Samantha often wished he were dead.   One day, when she was in the eighth grade, Paul Harrison expired in a drunken stupor. He was actually run down by a brewery truck. Her father would have seen that as a fitting end to his otherwise failed career. The money from the insurance settlement did permit Samantha and her mother to stay in the apartment and for Samantha to finish her schooling.

When in high school she had a torrid romance with a classmate which had been equally frustrating for them both. It wasn't until college that Samantha had lost her virginity. How she had envied her contemporaries who were extolling the ecstasies of co-ed sex. When Samantha surrendered her amateur status at the age of 19, she didn't feel that ecstasy. What she felt was physical pain of the penetration, a sense of self-induced violation, and a great sense of betrayal by her sisters-in-learning who had instilled in her expectations which her partner for the weekend hadn't fulfilled. In fact, the mostly drunken jerk had inexpertly and crudely attempted to make love to Samantha before he passed into a post coital sleep made all the sweeter for him by his heightened blood alcohol levels. Her date slept the sleep of the self indulgent. Samantha would not take another man to bed for another year.

She had a few friends in college, mostly among the theater arts crowd. Samantha dearly enjoyed role playing and was the kind of player who could project herself into a character and would become that character off stage as well as on. When she played the second lead in Hedda Gabbler, she even found herself entertaining lesbian interest in the woman playing opposite her. Lesbianism wasn't abhorrent to her, but in her normally ambivalent way of getting through life, neither was it a great attraction. Her one near experience had been with another student in

16

college.   They found themselves as the only two left in the dorm over a weekend, and at the other girl's suggestion they decided to share one room for the weekend for companionship.   They shared a lot of talking about childhood, men, aspirations, frustrations and desires.   As the evening mellowed they grew closer to one another, kissed and found it pleasurable.   Kissing led to groping and finally their naked bodies met in a bed designed to accommodate only one of them.   The constrictions of the space in which they found themselves and the fact that this was the first such experience for each of them, led to another night of arousal and unfulfilled expectations.

The adrenaline rush of knowing they could be discovered was probably more memorable than the pleasures of having another woman fondle and caress her knowing as a woman what could most pleasure a woman. It turned out to be Samantha's one and only homosexual encounter.   She often remembered it and when her relationships with men were somewhat disappointing, she seemed to recall this one night stand more fondly than at other times.

Samantha's one indulgence of vanity was her contacts.   As a youngster she had hated the eyeglasses that had been grafted onto her face at age 7.   She resented the bookish look they gave her as a teenager.   When she started to get seriously into theater, she learned a lot about make-up and what one could do with basic elements of human appearance.   Her contacts gave her the freedom to affect many poses including those in which she confidently wore eyeglasses fitted with clear glass instead of true lenses.

Samantha was a woman full of contradictions. She was considered a computer whiz at her work. But, it was computers that she still blamed for depriving her of a father when she had most needed him. She had hated Paul Harrison; but she had begun to understand the frustrations which he must have endured when he couldn't influence the direction and outcome of his life. The industrial age was supposed to make machines the servants of man. But, the information age was reversing that process.

It was a little past five when Samantha left the office complex on 16th Street. The sidewalks were crowded with young women in sneakers who either left their heels in their desk drawers, or carried them in plastic shopping bags suspended from their wrists, and the ubiquitous yuppiemen who wore suits from Brooks Brothers, and buttoned down oxford cloth shirts and respectable ties. The uniform was almost always the same, complete with fancy suspenders, which she supposed they gave out with BMW keys. Even in the depths of winter these yuppiemen could be seen in their shirtsleeves, dodging cars as they darted from their upscale office to some "in" watering hole to choke down their lunch while discussing the importance of the work they wished they had been doing, or the sports scene. Sam thought either conversation as dull as the other. Why was it that nobody under the age of 60 seemed to be able to discuss anything of real substance? Men all wanted to talk sports, politics and their view of what should be done to affect welfare reform and get rid of anything they determined was undesirable in their "new order." Women all seemed to be immersed in talk of men, children, and other women. Rarely did she find anyone of either sex who could stop in their track of trivial discourse to consider and respond to

18

matters relating to meaningful personal relationships or fulfillment as a thinking human being. Such was the state of contemporary society, thought Samantha. Everything was pre-packaged, pre-cooked, pre-sold, and pre-determined. Maybe they could come up with something pre-digested to save even more time. We have all bought into the sound bite as real life, and appearance as substance. The society that brought the world the A-bomb, Velcro, cell phones, frozen food and weight loss programs that didn't work, surely ought to be able to do better. Maybe in this 21st millennium. But we'd have to figure out what to do with all those Iraqis, first.

She mused these thoughts as she plowed through the crowd at the subway station on her way to 42nd Street. There stood the New York Public Library. Home to a burgeoning population of otherwise homeless people, the occasional researcher and those who actually stopped in to borrow a book, record, CD or tape. She quickly passed throuh security and smiled at one security guard who sat behind his severely undersized little desk in the lobby. She headed up to the business research area. There were elevators, but she preferred the stairs where she could choose her own company. Some of the elevator riders exuded the not-too-faint aroma of their lifestyle, and looked as if they might offer themselves to her for any perverted act she, or they, might conjure up. At least there was no STOP button on the stairway.

Samantha had gotten to know the library pretty well over the years. She customarily avoided the unhygienic public bathrooms and found her way to those reserved for Staff Only. She could exit the elevator and walk right into the ladies room before the under-worked security guard could question her.   He certainly wasn't going to risk following her in.   On her way back out, if he chastened her, she would just smile and say "Sorry - I really had to go." and make her escape into the adjacent stairwell. Since 9-11 it seemed that they had new guards every few weeks, so she rarely encountered the same one twice.

The business area had open shelved collections of magazines covering a wide range of topics.   The older copies in the library's holdings had been bound into buckram volumes.   It was in behind some antiquated bound volumes of Grocery Trade, that she found the two books she had previously stashed.   These had become important reference tools for her, but she didn't want either one to go missing (from her) nor did she want to sign either one of them out with her card.   *The Poor Man's James Bond* and the *Anarchist's Cookbook* were each first class primers for the would-be terrorist.   The former was chock full of hints about how the cops might work and what assets they could deploy, while the latter was full of how-to-do-it recipes for pipe bombs,   grenades and other homemade weapons of mass destruction.   She thought of the Russian emigree comedian, Yakov Smirnoff, who used to proclaim, "What a great country this is!"   Sure was. If you wanted to attack the system, just go to your friendly library which existed on government support, and ask for the information.   And as of 2009 it seemed that nothing had changed in that respect.

Samantha took her cached books and sought out a study carrel in the Government Documents section.   It appealed to her sense of humor to think that she did her research amongst the rarely-ever consulted collection of government documents which Congress had ordained shall

20

be distributed to specially designated libraries in every State.   She had no idea if the receipt and safekeeping of all this priceless rubbish brought with it a stipend to reimburse the city for the associated costs.   But she did know that the room had the feel of a sepulcher, and she could work without fear of interruption.   In all the time Samantha had been planning her attack, she had never taken a single note from the library, never borrowed a book, and never asked a question of anyone.   There was no record anywhere that she had ever visited this storehouse of information, and she was reasonably certain that nobody would recall her visits with any particularity. Even if they did, she was the female version of *jedermann* who looked like any one of a thousand other patrons, and not a soul in that library knew her name.   She was, in a word, transparent.

Something Samantha had noted in the televised trials of various celebrities was the introduction of evidence of telephone calls placed from one phone to another.   She knew it was obvious in the case of cellular phones where every connection is fully detailed on a bill.   But, she was uncertain about reproduction of logs of purely local connections.   Matlock, that old TV lawyer from Atlanta, was always producing these in Court.   She flipped quickly through the pages of one of the books and found what she had come for.   Basically, a telephone exchange is nothing more than a big computer and anything that goes into a computer can be retrieved until the time that it is trashed by plan or accident.   She certainly had no idea of blowing up the phone company's main frame, even if she knew where it was located.   Her decision was made.   No call or fax would emanate from her home or any venue associated with her.   She knew about voice stress analyzers, so she wouldn't want to communicate anything orally.   She also knew of the police ability to identify a voice, even if disguised, as well as the usual garden variety of devices such as caller ID, and automatic map-linking of caller ID to a location. If we could listen in on bin Laden's cell phone calls from 8,000 miles away somebody could surely intercept her communications. So, the answer was simple. Communications to her "pets" as she thought of them, would be only by fax, transmitted through an acoustic coupler, limited to not more than two minutes and sent from a now scarce coin phone, or by tapping into the phones of others.

Using somebody else's phone was pretty easy. Just by watching her own phone being installed, and having played around with it, she knew that only two wires were needed to run the standard non-electronic telephone. They were usually colored red and green and were referred to as the "tip" and "ring" leads.   Phones come into residences at a junction box which is usually on the back of the house. It is a breeze to open this box and using leads from her coupler to which she had affixed small alligator clips, she could be on and off of somebody's line before they could know it.   It was even easier in apartment houses or office buildings, if you could get access to the phone room. There you would find big boards with hundreds of leads coming in from telephone company trunks. They were often brought to plywood backing boards where they were stapled and then splayed out onto long bars of connectors where they were simply pushed into the crimping device to establish connection to the Key Switch Unit.   No matter how big and sophisticated these KSUs were, at some point they had to connect down to the good old fashioned phone line with the tip and ring leads.   If she could gain access

22

without being bothered by anyone then she could use the line and be gone in a flash.

The advantage of the office or commercial installation in addition to the ease of breaking into the phone line was that the room invariably had a door she could close, and very little security. Nobody would think to look in, and there was always a light and a 110-volt outlet. Sam had thought this all through very logically. She owned a small fax machine which could easily fit in a brief case. It was designed for use by people who live and work in their cars, and could be run off a car battery just like a cellular phone, or from regular electrical lines. The acoustic coupler was self contained and battery powered. Sam was totally mobile and anonymous in her communications ability. She liked the idea of using lines which could be identified as belonging to specific people and firms. If the police saw that the calls always came from coin phones, they would start looking for a pattern and watching some phones. She would have to drive all over hell and gone to make sure there was no patten they could determine. But, if she used phones traced to completely innocent people and firms, the cops would waste a lot of valuable time investigating one blind alley after another before they deduced that it was an interloper using the line. Police usually settle for the obvious. It isn't until their intellect is able to overwhelm their emotions, that they start really fitting the pieces together.

One of the cases she had read about, courtesy of the ATF, was of some guy in Arkansas who they finally caught after he set off about 5 or 6 bombs in the same town. Every Tuesday night a bomb would go off about 10 p.m., in a different part of town. Nobody had been hurt, the damage was slight, but it was a Federal case and a felony, and the Bureau of Alcohol, Tobacco & Firearms, a part of the Treasury Department, had been ordered to put a stop to this bombing spree. Agents looked at the pattern. There was none. But Arkansas has more than it's share of right wing militia types and the agent knew that Soldier of Fortune magazine was published there. A subpoena of all subscription records of the magazine produced only a couple of subscribers in this small town. With nothing more than that to go on, the ATF decided to put these two intellectuals under surveillance.

Voila! on the first Tuesday night, our hapless bomber leaves his home and drives into town. He realized that he was being followed. He drove around and tried evasion tactics. The ATF and local cops were closing in. He had a crude pipe bomb on the seat next to him, and he knew that setting off bombs wasn't a nice thing to do. So he tossed it out of the car window. As soon as the police saw the explosion they cornered this fellow and took him into custody. Turned out he was just a Good Old Boy who suffered from feelings that nobody paid him no mind. He didn't want to hurt anyone, but he did want to do something to make folks sit up and take notice. They did. He got sent up for a post-grad course in marking time at the government's expense. Samantha vowed that she wasn't going to be caught up by any such act of serendipity.

❸

About twelve miles away on the other side of town, Darryl Jones was just finishing up his report and getting ready to go home. Darryl was the senior terrorist specialist with the State Police. It seemed that a few days earlier persons unknown had managed to break into the enclosed storage yard of a local blasting company. There, in the midst of the rubble, was a solid concrete and steel bunker protected by a lock and collar that was virtually impenetrable. It was, of course, not totally safe. Whoever had broken in had simply cut their way through two perimeter fences of chain link and then managed to cut the lock out of its protective collar with an oxy-acetylene torch. What they were after and managed to get away with was 550 pounds of ammonium nitrate.

This was the same stuff that brought down the Murrah Federal Building in Oklahoma City. In addition to the ammonium nitrate, which was enough to blow up almost any major building in the city, these miscreants had run off with a box of blasting caps which were the triggers needed to do the job. The ATF was going particularly crazy over a spate of thefts of ammonium nitrate which had been steadily occurring since the attack on the World Trade Center. This particular lot of ammonium nitrate had already been mixed with fuel oil and had been pre-packed in fifty pound bags under the trade name ANFO. In the hands of any lunatic, these were bombs ready to go.

When the theft had been discovered, the local police had called in the Troopers, and because of the love affair between terrorists and explosives, it landed on Darryl's desk. Darryl had gone as far as he could go with the inquiry, which was to provide to ATF his list of local loonies who might be interested in this material. He had put out all the feelers he could, and came up with a big, fat zero. He was only too happy to turn this particular investigation over to ATF and sign off on it. Either they were going to make a bomb out of this, or they were going to use the stuff as fertilizer. But there is no restriction on the sale of fertilizer, therefore the assumption was that sooner or later, this stuff was going to blow up. When it did, he hoped to hell it wasn't on his watch, and he hoped it wasn't in his jurisdiction. In any event, the Feds were now involved, and they had more money, more staff, and more time, so God love 'em, let them go do the job.

It was in that frame of mind that Darryl decided not to bother to answer his phone, which was ringing off the hook. The caller got shunted to the usual voice-mail system where Darryl would collect the messages on Monday if he felt highly motivated. A caller completed a message and apparently hung up. A moment later, another caller came in. Darryl noticed that they both were coming in on his private, direct line. He answered neither call nor was he curious enough after a twelve-hour shift to check his voice mail. He didn't want his weekend to be disturbed by anything at this point. It wasn't but a minute later when the beeper on his belt started to vibrate, telling him that a message was coming in. He didn't recognize the number which flashed on the screen, and so he didn't return the call.

He signed his reports, threw them in the OUT basket for distribution, went down the hall to the washroom, cleaned up, logged out of the facility, and walked to his car. No more than three or four minutes had passed, and now the beeper on his belt started vibrating a second time. He grabbed the unit, took a look at the number, and noticed it was the same as before. "To hell with it." he thought. Darryl found his car, got into the vehicle and cranked it up when the beeper started going again. "Son of a bitch is really insistent." thought Darryl. He reached for his cell phone and placed a call to the number on the beeper.

"Darryl, that you?"

"Yeah, it's me, who's this?"

"Harry Mills. Look, Darryl, I know that you want to get the hell out of town, and I know it's Friday, I have to see you right away. It's very, very important."

"What's it all about, Harry?"

"I can's say on the air, Darryl, this is a face-to-face situation. What's your 20?"

"I'm just leaving the office."

"Okay, you headed towards town?"

"Yeah."

"How about you let me buy you some greaseburgers and I'll meet you at the diner?"

27

"You're on. My ETA is twelve to fifteen minutes depending on traffic and whether I use my little party lights."

"Use the friggin' party lights. I need to see you, and I need to see you now."

Darryl spotted Harry's car way at the back of the parking lot, and he slid the state vehicle in the adjoining slot. He rolled down the window and waited for the car-hop to come by to take his order. The old diner near the bridge still had car-hops serving some of the customers and it was a throw-back to Darryl's days as a college student. The food wasn't ever going to get four stars in any gastronomic guide, but tens of thousands of grown men and women who were presumed to know better, still frequented the place on a daily basis. Harry yelled across, "Don't bother to order - - I ordered enough of this stuff for the two of us, c'mon over and join me in my car."

Darryl let himself out, walked around, and got into the right-hand seat of Harry's car. He noticed that Harry, like a true urban sportsman, was a little bit short on housekeeping skills. He suspected that the last time that the car had been washed was when it was delivered by the dealer, and that was quite a few years ago. The car was basically held together by an awful lot of good luck and Bondo. Inside the car there were stains from the last thirty or forty meals that Harry had consumed while driving, as well as any hair and other debris left by his dog, who often was his traveling companion.

"What's up, Harry? It's Friday night."

"I know it's Friday, Darryl, and I hate to do this to you buddy, but this is a big one. I've got some asshole that wants to blow up the Expo Center."

"Shit man, why don't you report it to ATF? Going Boom is their problem."

"Yeah, well I thought about it. Let me run this by you. This jerk hasn't exactly said he's going to blow it up. He hasn't used the word explosive, nor has he used the word explosion or bomb. You know what the deal is with ATF, they can't come into a case until either a explosion is imminent or it's already happened. But, if I wait until it's happened, I might as well start lookin' for a new job or plan on winning the lottery for my retirement fund. I can't afford to let the damn thing go off. I need your help and I need it bad."

"Does Carly know about it?"

"Oh sure, he knows about it. This son of a bitch sent the faxes to Carly's executive palace fax machine, and that big mouth Tabatha has read the damn thing. Carly, of course, has done his usual act. He's thrown the whole thing on me, and now I'm stuck in the situation that I gotta find some son of a bitch, who I don't even know who it is, who's threatened to disrupt one of the biggest shows in the city and I'm gonna have everybody on my ass if I screw up."

"Wow," a suddenly impressed Darryl just stroked his chin and looked steadily at Harry Mills who was starting to sweat profusely. "What are you gonna do about it, Harry?"

"What am I gonna do about it?" yelled Harry. "For Christ's sake, I'm not a cop anymore, remember? I run a junior police force that guards a bunch of conventioneers and trade show people. I can't go out there and start arresting people and shaking people down, and irritating the living shit out of them. That's your job, dickhead."

"Oh, no it isn't, pal. Nobody's given me the case. I don't go out soliciting business. We got enough goddamn lunatics around that I don't have to go looking for new clientele. My specialty? Yeah, it's terrorism. But this person hasn't said they're going to launch a terrorist attack. Do you have copies of the faxes with you?"

"Yeah, yeah, I got 'em right here." Harry fished into a manila envelope and extracted several pieces of paper, which he perfunctorily handed to the unhappy Darryl. "Here, read 'em and weep. The son of a bitch says that he's gonna take down the Electronika Internationale Show. You know what that means to the city? You got any fuckin' idea? It's worth a hundred million bucks in revenue. You think the mayor's gonna sit still on this one? You think the governor's gonna sit still on this one? Every fuckin' sissy-pants politician in this town is gonna be screaming for my fat ass and yours if we don't get this thing taken care of. So, you gonna help me, or am I gonna march downtown to the newspaper?"

"Well okay, Harry, of course I'm going to help you. I just wanted to make sure that this was being handled in an appropriate fashion. Has it gone to the City P.D. or to the Office of Homeland Security?"

"The P.D.? What do you want me to take it to them for? This is not a stolen car. This isn't some two-bit dime-packin' hustler who got offed in the projects. This is a certified lunatic who wants to blow up my fuckin' show, and I'm not gonna take a chance with the boys in blue screwin' it up. And I can't call HomeSec. First thing we know there's a press release out, we're at code orange and the show goes down the drain. We need your department."

"Okay Harry, what can you give me to go on?" As he said it, Darryl opened a little flip-notebook and took out his Bic to make some notes.

"You can close the pen, pal. I don't know shit. I don't know who this person is, I don't know where this person is--I don't know anything about him."

"Well, where were the faxes sent from, Harry?"

"I don't know. Take a look at the top of the fax. There's no sending machine identification."

"Oh shit," muttered Darryl. "Well what about the name Sam? Do you got any disgruntled former employees named Sam?"

"Of course I've got former employees named Sam. First of all, all of our friggin' former employees are disgruntled--if they were gruntled, they'd still be working with us. Not only that, but probably half of the bastards are named Sam, John, or Jim. But think about this, there isn't one of those bozos with enough brains to

31

write a cogent, English-language message, or to send it, like this guy has, so that we got no way of tracking it."

Darryl thought for a moment. "Maybe we do have a way of tracking it. Did you think about having your fax machine print out the connection log? Maybe it was sent from a machine that had its phone number in there somehow."

"No shit, Dick Tracy. Of course I did. You know what it says? G3. Just means that whoever sent the son of a bitch sent it from a modern fax machine. That should limit it to maybe a million people in the immediate area."

"Well how do you know that this guy's in the area, Harry?"

"Well, that's a good point. You know, I don't know. I'm just making an assumption. Personally, I wish they'd go blow up the goddamn Moscone Center in San Francisco or go try and blow up McCormick in Chicago. I don't need 'em in my back yard. You know you're a friggin' genius. If I knew who the hell this person was, or I could send a message back, I'd pay the son of a bitch to take it out of town and get rid of the problem."

"Okay, okay. Who else down at the Expo Center knows about this threat?"

Harry laughed. "Who else knows? I told you that Tabatha read the friggin' fax, okay? She can't keep her mouth shut for two seconds. I'll be lucky if any of those bastards show up to work after Monday because once they all hear about it they're gonna think the whole building is going to go boom. I only gotta worry about the Security staff. Carly's gonna have to get off his ass and get his people to start hiring an awful lot more people, because those maintenance guys, they ain't gonna want to work in a building they think is going to blow up. The secretaries don't want to get blown up. There ain't any of us who are really keen on the idea of getting blown up, *comprende?"*

The waitress came by and affixed a tray to the left hand door of the car, dropped off two greaseburgers and a milk shake, came around, and delivered an equal order to Darryl's side. The two guys choked down their meal and started sucking up their milk shakes in total silence. Finally, Darryl had something to say.

"Harry, I'm gonna do what I can to help you. I've gotta run it by my chief; you know that. I'll call Wallace over at ATF and see what they can do to help us. I don't know that we can stop this guy. How long do we have on this?"

"Five fuckin' days. They start the move-in for Electronika in five days. And shortly after that, I'm gonna have a hundred thousand visiting firemen from all over the country schleppin' their buns through my halls and not suspecting a thing. You got any idea where an over-the-hill ex-cop who's now a security chief for an Expo Center can find a job if his last one blew up on his watch?"

"Naw, come on, Harry--I don't know. And the joint is not gonna blow up on your watch or anybody else's. We're gonna find the son of a bitch and we're gonna put him down before he can take down your show.

Wallace is the chief now over at ATF, and hopefully he'll feel like he owes me one from his last case, 'cause I gave him an awful lot of stuff that we had on the theft of the ammonium nitrates. We're obviously gonna need some sophisticated backup. I'm gonna get the phone company to give us a printout on all Caller IDs coming in to your fax number, so I need a list of all the numbers on which you receive faxes. I'm gonna want to put a voice-tap on your line and on Carly's, and we're going to need your written authority to do that. I want you to come over to my place tomorrow morning about, oh, eight or eight-thirty. I want to show you our mug shots of our own home-grown lunatics so you can tell me if you recognize any of them. My thought is that maybe one of these creeps has worked at your facility under a stiff name. I'm also a little concerned about the references to your family and to Carly's, and I think we better put taps on all lines coming into your pad and his. That would also include any cell phones that you or Carly are using. Is that okay with you?"

"Yeah, sure, you know. That's fine. While you're at it, maybe I should prepay for some funeral expenses?"

"Look, Harry. This ain't necessarily the easiest case in the world to solve, but every one of these jerks makes a mistake that we finally catch up to them with. You know, just think of the guy that's accused of setting off that bomb in Oklahoma City. We just happened to catch him because he gets stopped driving a car that's over the speed limit with no license tags. And he's sitting in a jail in some bum-fuck little town, and we had him all the time and didn't even know it. This person's going to screw up, and we're going to get him. You can take that to

34

the bank."

"Okay, okay, Darryl. I'm beginning to feel better. You understand now why I didn't want this to go out over the air?"

"Sure I do. I understand where you're coming from, Harry. But if it's all the same to you, I've got my own life to lead too, and I've got a hot date tonight."

"Oh, does Sally know about that?"

"Ah," said Darryl. "I see you're not very up on my private life. Whether Sally knows or doesn't know has now become irrelevant since the twenty-first of last month. That's when she took the kids, the dog, the boat, the house, the bank-accounts, the jewelry, and anything else that was worth a shit and told me that it was hers, and got the judge to agree with her. So I am now divorced, single, and the proud owner of one television set, some old tape recordings, and my own clothing. How's that grab you?"

"Oh shit, I'm sorry. I really stepped into it, and I'm sorry I asked."

"Oh well, don't be. You know those things happen, and I didn't mean to lay a bum trip on you. Anyway, I've got a date with a young lady tonight that I really think a lot of, and I really don't want to miss it. So I'll see you tomorrow morning, let's say eight-thirty, my place. Use the side door, security code to enter will be 8144. Got it?"

"Yep. See you then."

4

Samantha laid down her pencil and sat staring at the wall. The last bits of information which she needed to put her plan into operation had now fallen into her lap. She knew when to attack the Electronika show, she knew why she wanted to attack it, and now she knew exactly how to attack it in a way that would ensure both success and escape. There were a couple of things that she wanted to do before she started the final steps. Samantha knew that she must have caused some nervous reaction over at the Expo Center, but she wanted to know what Harry Mills was up to and she also wanted to know that her theories concerning disruptive devices would work. In which case, she needed to run a controlled test. Tonight she'd check out Harry Mills' home to see what sort of activity was going on, and in the morning she would run the tests.

She returned the books to their hiding place, checked around to make sure that nobody was in the Government Documents section, then took the paper on which she had written her notes and went to the public use computer bank in the library. Here, she selected one particular computer terminal which was set at an angle to the others in such a position that it was unlikely that anyone could see the monitor other than her. With a few keystrokes entered, Samantha brought up on screen all of the information she had obtained in more than a year of research and planning. She had all of the plans for the Expo Center, all of the information on the Electronika show, including staffing requirements, past job advertisements, exhibitor lists--including addresses and fax numbers, and the plans of all of the utilities coming into the giant center. All of this information and more had been stashed at no cost on computers owned by the city, and in such a manner that it was invisible to anyone coming on-line who didn't know how she had partitioned the drive and renamed it. Of course, all of the files had been encrypted and password-protected. Even if they found the files, nobody would be able to know who had put them there. Samantha often wondered how many other people had managed to finagle the city's computers as she had done. She didn't think she was a computer whiz-kid; but, it really wasn't that difficult. And, it sure beat having incriminating evidence laying around her own home.

For Samantha it had always been a toss-up between two plans of attack. One involved personal appearance on-site and the other one was entirely remote-control. She just couldn't go with the idea of not being available to see exactly what she had wrought. For that reason she adopted Plan One. Plan Two had been much simpler in that she knew exactly where the main water lines into the Expo Center were located. It would have been a fairly simple matter to drill into the lines and insert into them automatic feeders which would dispense a noxious but colorless agent in the water. Within hours of the show opening, she would have thousands of people retching and heaving throughout the facility. It wouldn't take very long for the show to close down. But what would that do for her? She needed to be there to see the panic and she needed to know that everything was going just as she had planned it. It was the same sort of reasoning that led her to abandon the idea of simply advising all of the exhibitors that she was planning to attack the show. What exhibitor in their right mind was going to put their personnel and their expensive exhibit at risk in a building like the Expo Center?

But, if she did this, and if that worked, then the show wouldn't be held at all and she wouldn't have been able to see the results of her endeavors. "No", thought Samantha, "far better that I do it with my own hands in my own way." Having entered the last bits of data into her secret files, she exited the computer program and walked casually over to the recycling area trash-bins on the floor where the city had thoughtfully provided a paper-shredder over one of them. She took the papers on which she had made her notes in the Government Documents section and casually fed them into the shredder. Good-bye, evidence.

Daylight Savings Time was in effect and it was still bright daylight when she left the library about 6:15. Samantha walked towards the restaurants near the library, planning to get a bite to eat before the night's labors. She stopped, bought the newspaper from a curb-side vending rack and whiled away an hour or so with her sandwich and Coke. She had only one activity for tonight, and that was to check out Harry's home. For that, she preferred to wait until the wee hours of the morning, and being fed and otherwise satisfied, Samantha left the restaurant and started to walk home. She lived about two-and-a-half miles from the downtown area, and as it was still light, and she could stay on main streets. She thought that she would enjoy a brisk walk in the gentle breeze of that warm evening. She reached home about 9:00 p.m.

Samantha checked her answering machine. No

messages. She checked her mail. Nothing of any interest. She checked the television schedule, same thing there, nothing of any interest. She kicked off her shoes, loosened her clothes, and sat down with a bag of chips and one of her favorite videos. She couldn't get enough of True Lies, and Shwarzenegger and the high-tech attacks on the government. The only thing was, she was rooting for the wrong side. She watched the film all the way through and dozed off for about an hour or so. Her alarm clock rang at 1:00 a.m. and Samantha quickly turned it off, adjusted her clothing, and quietly left her apartment unnoticed.

Her little car sputtered to life on the first try. It was one of those four-bangers which she had bought from a rental company about three years before. She loved the car--what she didn't love was that it had an annoying habit of parts falling out of it in rapid succession. She had sent off some letters to Detroit asking what sort of quality control they had back in 2005, but nobody had ever bothered to answer her letters. In any event, Samantha consoled herself that it was cheaper to make the occasional repair than it was to buy a new car. On what she was getting paid, buying a new car was a long way off. She knew the way to Harry's house, had driven by it many times before. This evening she drove by slowly and quietly about 1:20 a.m. and took note that the lights in the downstairs front room were on, as well as the lights in the second floor front room. She had to assume that the second-floor front room was the bedroom and that the downstairs front-right room had to be either a living room, den, or dining room. In any event, she assumed the master bedroom would be in the back of the house, and therefore lights on in two rooms meant that one or more persons in that house were up and concerned about something at twenty minutes after one.   There was no evidence of company or any other car parked in the driveway or near Harry's home.

Samantha took a right turn and headed towards midtown. She would be back in another hour or so. Four times during that night Samantha drove past Harry Mills' house, taking note of the lights that were on and furtively searching to see if she could discern any activity through the window. She dared not stop nor walk down the road. People in New York just didn't go walking in residential neighborhoods in the middle of the night.

The next morning Samantha left her apartment again about 10:00 a.m. and headed toward the lower Hudson Valley.   Proceeding northbound, Samantha tore into her breakfast which consisted of a can of Diet Coke and an Ultra Slim-Fast Peanut Butter Crunch bar. When a friend had suggested she try these diet bars, she said that she thought they were made from sawdust and glue encased in some sort of chocolate coating;   but they had became addicting very quickly.

She laughed once when she had read the panel on the box where the manufacturer had written "ATTENTION: These bars are incredibly delicious. Please don't overeat. Remember, the purpose is to help you keep your weight down. Drink two glasses of water or diet beverage with each bar to help you satisfy your hunger." Yeah, sure they don't want you to overeat. She couldn't imagine that anybody at the company would care if you ate fifteen of these suckers a day. In fact, she had once gotten through two days with nothing but diet bars and hadn't noticed any loss of weight whatsoever. The big advantage of these bars was that they were almost identical in every respect to bars which were sold by specific diet regimens and nutrition plans that charged users three or four times as much for the same junk. She had tried them all, and found the Peanut Butter Crunch was the one she really liked. It not only felt like it was sticking to her ribs, but it provided many moments of entertainment trying to dig the impacted crud out of her fillings after she'd eaten them. The sun was shining, it was about 78 degrees, her radio was blaring, and for once the car was running like a real automobile instead of a washing machine.

Within 45 minutes she swung onto the secondary road that would lead her up to a nearby lake. What appealed to her was the scenery and that there were so many areas that were not only beautiful but away from prying eyes. Within another hour, she pulled off at a real-estate sign that was offering some 50 acres for sale with lake frontage. There was a clearly marked driveway or car trail into the property, and Samantha eased her car off the road and into the lane.

About 300 yards down, behind a grove of trees, she stopped, turned off the car, and sat on the trunk of the vehicle, looking toward the road for several minutes to determine if she could see the cars going by and if they could see her. After a while, satisfied that no eyes were focused in her direction, Samantha took a small overnight case from the back of her car, and walked the remaining few hundred yards down to the little lake.

In this area, the lake was very shallow and hence there were neither boaters or tubers around. There being no residential areas on either side of this parcel of land for sale, there were no kids playing there, and the only sounds that she could hear were the occasional birds taking flight from the trees. She knew that this part of the area tended to be snake infested and she looked carefully at the rocks before she selected a place to sit. From her experiences as a Girl Scout, she knew that snakes loved to sun themselves on rocks and that rocks retain the heat which the snakes need. She satisfied herself that the place she had selected was not designed to set her up with a rapid bite in the rear end, and she opened her case and started to work.

Samantha drew from the case a small brown glass laboratory bottle, the stopper of which was secured by a leak proof screw top. She was familiar with the warning label printed in bright red on the bottle. She selected an olive clamp, which could be used to retrieve a small object and laid it to one side.

Samantha then took a plastic dish about one and a half inches deep and four inches square from the case and filled it from the lake with cold water. The dish had a hole in the bottom, close to one end, which Samantha had pierced with an awl and then covered with waterproof adhesive tape on the inside of the dish. She set this dish on a nearby flat rock.

At the sound of a rustle in the bushes, Samantha froze like a deer and stood motionless and silent for fully half a minute before she concluded it was only a small animal leaving the scene.

She carefully opened the bottle and laying the

cap aside, inserted the olive clamp and used it to engage a small cube of white chalky material about one quarter inch in size. With the bottle held next to the plastic dish she withdrew the stuff and in one seamless movement immersed it immediately into the dish of water. She quickly but carefully replaced the cap on the bottle and placed it back in her case. Samantha took her case and placed it about six feet away from her, then using a long nose pliers she gingerly pulled back the adhesive tape which she removed from the dish. Then Samantha moved back to watch the reaction.

The water started to drip from the dish and trickle down over the flat rock. It took about 4 minutes for the water to recede to a level that exposed the top of the cube. It seemed more like an hour. But, as the cube of material was exposed to the air, it started to smoke and created a great amount of smoke and heat. As the remaining water in the container leaked out it exposed more of the cube, which finally burst into flame and burned brightly. Samantha waited a full 10 minutes before she gingerly inspected the plastic pan. The material had burned a hole right through the bottom of the pan and left a burn mark on the rock.

Next she repeated the experiment with a similar pan, although she first enlarged the bung hole on it to permit the water to flow out more quickly. She filled the pan again with cold water and set it on the rock in such fashion that it tilted downward toward the bung hole, which would permit a faster and more complete disposal of the water. Samantha drew two cubes of this volatile material from the brown jar and observed the reaction when she let the water out of the pan. She made careful mental notes of the exothermic reactions she was observing.

Finally Samantha set up one experiment wherein she deposited several chunks of the material and covered the dish with papers immediately after she pulled up the adhesive tape. The water ran out quickly, the volume of steam and smoke was impressive and the papers burst gloriously into bright flame. Most of the container was consumed in the fire. Aha! That was the formula. Samantha carefully brushed away the evidence of her scientific investigation and threw any remaining debris into the lake. Although she realized there was no real chance her presence could have been detected, what she was doing there, could relate to events about to unfold in the city, so Samantha carefully policed the area, to make sure there was absolutely nothing there to connect her with this location. She retraced her steps to her waiting car, turned it around, and slowly exited the road heading back to the highway and home..

On her way, Samantha stopped to use a coin-phone to check her messages at home. It griped her to have to blow more than two dollars to make a call just down to town but she did not want to use a credit card. There were no messages--there was no reason to hurry home. Before returning, Samantha would stop to enjoy the buffet dinner at a lodge which always featured her favorite of locally grown turkey. The price was half of what it cost in the city and the quality was better. Samantha was playing for time. She did not want to get back until dark because she wanted to visit her friend Harry again to see how things were going at the Mills' residence.

About eight o'clock in the evening, Samantha left the park and slowly but deliberately headed back toward town, keeping well within the speed limit at all times. The warm evening breezes blew through her car and she reveled in the sound of the cicadas who set up quite a symphony in the rural areas at that time of year. It was about nine-thirty when she finally got to the city and the last rays of daylight had evaporated into night. She drove directly to Harry's home where she noticed that there were no lights on whatsoever, nor was there any evidence of a vehicle near Harry's house. On a hunch, Samantha decided to drive over to the Expo Center, and went around to the rear of the complex to the entrance near the loading dock. She was quite certain that Harry and the other big shots would park there to avoid a long walk from the public parking areas. She was right on target. As she drove along the road which bordered the employee area, she could see in the glare of the sodium vapor lamps the outline of Harry's car. She was pleased to know that he was now hard at work on what should have been a day off. She'd had a pleasant day in the country and accomplished quite a bit. She had no idea what Harry had been up to.

❺

Harry Mills sat at his desk. The light from the fluorescent tubes cast an eerie pall over the entire room. He had often thought that fluorescent lighting tended to flatten out objects until they assumed surrealistic appearances, especially when he was dead tired. Dead tired was what Harry was at that moment. He had been up most of the night desperately searching the attic of his mind trying to think who in the hell this Sam could be who had turned his life upside down. In the morning he had met Darryl as agreed, and for an hour-and-a-half had gone through the most amazing collection of pictures of people of all backgrounds who were known as terrorists or would-be terrorists. Harry failed to recognize a single one of them. In fact, he wanted to quit about halfway through but Darryl wouldn't let him. He had asked Darryl about a few of the men who seemed to be dressed in business suits with plain white shirts and very neat bow ties. He assumed that they all belonged to one particular group or order.

In fact they were all thought to be members of the Nation of Islam, and although there was no evidence whatsoever that any of the followers of Minister Farrakhan had ever engaged in a violent act against the government or any other organization, they were being made the object of intense police scrutiny and targeted by almost every police agency in the country for infiltration. Should the Nation of Islam abandon its ways of peaceful coercion, and embark upon a program of destruction then the forces of law were poised to come down upon them with the wrath of the righteous. Remembering the lessons of the past, it was well-considered that it was merely a few small steps from outrageous rhetoric of hatred to taking up arms against the objects of one's hatred. And when it came to spewing hatred in contemporary America, there had been no more vitriolic spokesperson, then Minister Farrakhan.

It was now 11:30 on Saturday morning. Harry had left Darryl with his wonderful collection of family photographs and had headed back toward his home for lunch with Mary. She knew he'd been up most of the night and she knew he was worried. In fact, she hadn't seen Harry looking so haggard since the problem with the D.A.R. convention. Harry turned his rambling wreck of a car into the driveway at 11:52 a.m. He entered the house and, as was his custom, headed for the kitchen in a mindless exercise of opening the refrigerator door and taking inventory. He wasn't particularly hungry, he just always went to the fridge, and always looked for something to eat. Mary usually made certain there was some sort of snack food toward the front of one of the shelves about chest-high so he wouldn't have to look too far.

Harry hardly noticed Mary sitting quietly at the table in the dining nook. He grabbed an apple off the shelf, bit into it, and let the door to the fridge close as he turned around. Harry spied her sitting quietly with her hands folded in an unusual sort of posture. "What's up Hon?"

Mary looked up at him like a puppy-dog expecting to be hit. Her eyes were rimmed with red. She looked as though she had been crying. "Harry, something's going on. Please, Dear, sit down and tell me what's happening. I have to know, or I'm going to go crazy."

48

"What happened, Honey?"

Mary held out her hands to Harry, who took them in his as he sat down. She looked him square in the eyes and said, "Honey, the phone has rung seven times while you have been out this morning. Each time I have answered it within two or three rings, and each time the caller has hung up without saying a word. Now I know something's going on. You've got to tell me. Why is somebody calling our house? Why are they trying to torture you and me?"

Harry thought for a moment, took a controlled breath, "Did you hear anything?"

"No--I told you, the caller said nothing. All I heard was a hang-up, a click."

"What about background noises? Did you hear anything like a train, cars, buses, radios, television sets, anything?"

Mary played with her bottom lip between her thumb and index finger as she thought. Then, slowly, "No, nothing that I'd really recognize as being specific. In a couple of instances, it did sound like automobile traffic or trucks going by, but sometimes I don't think it was in all of the calls. Why? What should I have heard?"

"I don't know. I don't know who this is--but, I do know that I've got to find him." Harry slid from the booth and walked back to the fridge, where he grabbed a beer, turned around, and said, "You want one too?"

Mary shook her head. Harry pulled back the tab on his beer, took a long guzzle as he walked back to the dinette and slid in opposite his wife.

"Okay Mary, here's the score. I'm not going to hold anything back from you. Yesterday, some nitwit sent a fax to Carly's office saying that they were going to disrupt the Electronika show. Carly is in his usual frame of mind. He laid it all on me. Whoever this is, I have no idea, other than that the guy's name is Sam. What else I can't tell you. Sam has made sure that everybody at the Expo Center knows because it's gone to Carly's fax, which means that Tabatha is going to run her mouth to anybody she can find. The fax was sent from a fax machine that isn't traceable. We don't know the phone number from which the call was made. I can get one of my buddies at the Feds to try to get the information from the phone company, but things being how they are, the phone company's not going to cough up the information easily. And I'm not sure it's going to make a whole hell of a lot of difference.

"I got hold of Darryl Jones, and in fact it was Darryl I was meeting with this morning. The little bastard didn't really want the case, but I had to explain to him that if this screwball carries out his threat, then Darryl's ass, mine, and a lot of other people are going to be squarely on the grill. So now Darryl has offered to help. Carly, of course, has done a flit and is off on some social engagement. I've got more than three hundred tractor-trailers coming in, in the next three days to set up for this show. I've got a crew working for me with a collective IQ slightly higher than their waist size. And I've got a hundred thousand or more visitors coming to the Center at the end of the week.

"My problem is very simple. I only have to find Sam and stop him before he takes down the show. Now I got a couple of little problems to solve along the way. One, I don't know who the hell Sam is, I don't know where he is, I don't know what he looks like, I don't know how he plans to take down the show--and I have to hope to hell that the son of a bitch calls or sends more faxes. I did arrange with Darryl to go ahead and put taps on all the phones that are important at the Center and I have given him permission to put a tap on our line here, so maybe that was what you heard this morning with the hang-ups." Harry was looking at Mary while he said this. She knew it was a lie, just as he knew. They would never test the tap by calling the number. And if Darryl had ordered it, and they did test it by ringing the number, they would have asked her to identify herself, they would have told her that the tap was being installed. In any event, she could see that Harry was clearly worried. She took his free hand in both of hers, squeezed it lightly, "Harry, what are we going to do?"

"What are we gonna do? Well, I don't know that *we* are going to do anything. I think probably the best thing for you right now would be for you to go visit your mother in Ohio for a few days. In the meantime, I'm going to do whatever the hell I can think of to try and find this son of a bitch."

Without any warning, Mary stood up, slammed her hand flat on the table and yelled, "Bullshit! I'm not going off to Ohio. You think I'm going to run away because some son of a bitch is going to cause a problem for my husband? Tell me this, Harry, is somebody trying to

51

kill you or me?"

"No! That's not the case at all."

"Okay, then screw 'em. I'm staying right here with you. Tell me what you want me to do and I'll do it. But Mamma doesn't need me--you do, and this is where I'm staying." She pulled Harry from his perch, and as he rose from the bench of the dinette, she clasped him to her and they embraced slowly and passionately. Perhaps more passionately than they had in many years. There's something about the adrenaline of danger that raises the emotional level of all reactions. Mary knew there wasn't much she could do, other than provide a safe and secure environment for Harry. She was sorry that she had mentioned the phone calls, but they had really rattled her. On the other hand, she needed to know what was troubling him. Now that she knew, she felt totally helpless.

6

At 12:20 p.m. the telephone at Brice Youngmann's house rang. Brice had installed distinctive ringing, so that he knew it was the office. "Youngmann here."

"Hi, Brice, this is Bill Thomas, and I'm D.O. today. I thought you should know we just got a signal from the Director's office that Rosebud may be in town at the end of next week for this Electronika Show."

"Balls." Brice didn't need the Vice President and a bunch of Secret Service men showing up on his turf while he had a thousand other things to deal with in the normal course of events. "What the hell's it all about?"

"I dunno. But I do know that the big Electronika Show is coming next week. Maybe he's coming to make some opening remarks."

"Okay, do me a favor and see what you can find out. Is there anything that they're requesting us to do today that I need to take action on?"

"No, nothing that I can see."

"Okay then, just keep me posted. I'm going to be doing some errands this afternoon and check the machine later tonight. I'll have my beeper on. Just contact me if need be. If it's this problem give me a Code 100." Brice wasn't particularly crazy about a Vice-Presidential visit. The President and the Vice-President both liked to pop in and out of New York from time to time. There were excellent media facilities for all the photo opportunities. It was only about a short ride from the base to any place they wanted to go in the city.

What a visit from the Vice President or President did mean was that there would be several executive 747s coming in and a fleet of limousines and a battalion of protection for the President, the Vice President, and their entourage. Everybody knew the responsibility for the protection of the President and the Vice-President and their families lay with the Secret Service. What people may not realize is that the Secret Service were generally augmented by agents from the Bureau, and local law enforcement agencies. A Presidential visit was tantamount to a full-alert status. If the Vice-President was coming in five or six days, then he knew that the advance team would be here within the next day or so and that the initial arrangements would be well in place, at least three days before his arrival. In fact, they liked to make the arrangements as far in advance as possible so that all available personnel who might possibly be needed could be alerted and given assignments.

The workload in Brice's office wasn't at that critical stage at this time. Things had been relatively cool as far as he was concerned. If anything, the local office of the FBI was proceeding at what he thought to be a rather comfortable pace. He would just as soon that it stayed that way.

Samantha sat on the patio of one of the restaurants and finished her beer and tacos. She had been sitting on the deck for almost an hour, just watching the traffic flow by and planning the rest of her week. She was remarkably calm, considering that she was about to wreak havoc upon one of the most important trade shows in the Western world. She had no idea that the Vice President of the United States might be among the crowd the day that she was there.

❼

3:00 p.m. Harry Mills let himself into the now deserted Expo Center. His assignment detail for the day had posted two men to do their walking tours in the facility. He found one of them having lunch in a little office adjacent to the loading dock. Harry hoped the other one was at least getting out and walking around to check the doors and windows. As he looked into the small office Harry asked, "Everything cool?"

"Sure thing, Chief. No problems," was the response. Harry continued on his way to the executive suite on the top floor. Using his master keys he let himself in and went directly to the fax machine on the console behind Tabatha's desk. There, waiting for Harry Mills, was what he hoped for and dreaded most. A fax from his nemesis, Sam. He carefully tore the fax off and went to the copy machine. He switched it on. Harry wanted to make several copies of this fax for distribution--he didn't want to take a chance that his copy could get lost. As in the previous fax, there was no indication of the sending transmitter, and no indication of the number from which it had been sent. Harry did engage the fax machine to print out a transmission receipt ticket for this fax and determined that it had been sent about an hour before. At least this was something to go on, with the taps in place. Harry read the fax as he was waiting for the copy machine to warm up. It had been generated by a word processor to a printer which may or may not be identifiable. The fax said, "Hello Harry: I hope you are enjoying your day off. I noticed that you were up most of last night, and I'm sure that Mary is getting concerned by now. Be a good boy and try to calm her fears. It isn't you, Harry, that I'm after. I know this is difficult for you, but there's absolutely nothing you can do to prevent me from short-circuiting the Electronika show. If I were you, I'd pay very careful attention to all those trucks which start to unload tomorrow. Catch you later. Sam."

"Son of a bitch," Harry muttered to no one other than himself. He made six copies of the fax, took one and placed it in an envelope which he sealed and wrote "Private: For Carlton Bentwood Only." He let himself into Carly's office and left the envelope on the seat of his Imperial Majesty's chair. Harry closed the door to Carly's office and seated himself at Tabatha's desk in the Reception area. From this vantage point, he could see through the glass wall should anybody come within earshot. He drew from his wallet a card with a series of phone numbers on it, one of which was Darryl Jones' home number. Three rings, and Darryl answered the phone.

"Yeah?"

"Hi, Harry here. Got another fax, Darryl."

"Okay, can you read it to me?"

"Yeah Darryl. My line is clean and in fact this particular line I'm on has a tap on it from our friends, but what do you think about your end?"

"I don't think there's any problem Harry, go ahead."

Harry read the text of the fax. Darryl didn't answer immediately. After a couple of seconds, he said, "Well, what do you think you're gonna do?"

"What the fuck am *I* gonna do? I told you, Darryl, this is what are *we* gonna do, goddammit!"

"Yeah, yeah, yeah. Listen, take it easy, will you? Okay Harry, the first thing I'm gonna do is have you fax a copy of that to my office. Got the number?"

"Yeah."

"Okay, the next thing I want to do is run a full background check on every former and current employee of your organization, let's say for the last two or three years. Can you get those personnel files to me today?"

"Naw, I don't think I can, without getting a lot of people very nervous. I probably can't get them until Monday morning at 8:30."

"Okay, I'll have a gofer at your office at 8:45 Monday morning. We need the usual information and any incident reports you have concerning any of them. Harry, that reminds me. You still got incident reports on file on anyone you've apprehended or ejected from your facility?"

"Yeah, you know I do. I have to keep 'em because every one of those creeps threatens to sue us."

"Okay, fine. Let me have those going back a couple of years. You know, we're not certain that this is a former employee, are we?"

"No, the only thing that we know for certain is that we don't know a goddamn thing for certain. I got a bunch of semis starting to come in here at 0700 tomorrow. I need some help on the loading docks. How about sending me some of your whiz-kids and maybe a couple of your puppy-sniffers?"

"Okay, you got 'em. I'll have them there at 0700. What do you think that we might be lookin' for?"

"Darryl, listen to me and try to understand this one simple concept. I'm gonna say it real slow. I have no fuckin' idea. Got it?"

"Got it. See you tomorrow."

Sean Casey was always the caricature of the Irish cop. True, he had flat feet and flaming red hair, but he was no dumb Mick. As chief of security for Electronika, Casey was responsible for securing not only the asset value of hundreds of millions of dollars worth of property, but also protecting the personal well-being of more people in one location than live in most small towns. Electronika drew more visitors than the Super Bowl. Bigger than the quadrennial nominating conventions, this year it may have the added prestige of a keynote address from none other than the Vice President of the United States. When he was coming up through the ranks in the Baltimore police department, Casey had worked in almost every one of the stations. He had even spent a tour working on the harbor patrol. He had come up against some of the toughest and nastiest human beings that God ever placed on the face of the Earth. And when he was brought in by the owners of the Electronika show to head up their security department, at a salary of three times what he could make on the cops, he knew he had to say yes. It was a good job. He had a nice, comfortable office with new furniture, something he would never achieve at a police department, and his own secretary. There were no bars on the windows and no foul-smelling miscreants sitting on benches as he walked into his office each day. When he traveled, he usually flew First Class, or as he really liked to do, in one of the company's own jets.

Casey had conferred with the owners of similar shows in Japan, Brazil, and Germany, all on the company payroll and with full company permission. This was big business. The average exhibitor would be paying about fifty bucks a square foot for exhibit space, which meant that the tiniest exhibit, which would be a ten by ten foot booth containing a booth with a hundred square feet, cost about five thousand dollars just for the rental of the booth. The exhibitors can add to that the cost of fitting out the booth with their exhibit, and carpeting, and other amenities and the cost of transporting their exhibit, and their personnel and the hotel bills and labor charges for the week of the show.

For even the smallest exhibitors, the cost probably had to exceed nine or ten thousand dollars. When you started to think about the exhibitors who shipped in massive two-story exhibits covering a thousand square feet or more, it was obvious that these companies were spending hundreds of thousands of dollars each year to attend and exhibit at the Electronika show. They had a right to expect that their property and their persons would be secure. "Red" Casey was the guy they reposed confidence in to provide total protection. In fact, the security of this show was so good that there had never been a single incident. But, that was before the Electronika Internationale 2009. And, before events put Samantha Harrison on a collision course with the Vice President of the United States.

Samantha was a little annoyed with herself. She had stopped to get the Sunday newspaper which was on the street by noon Saturday but forgot that they didn't post the lottery numbers until after the drawing which was held at 11 p.m. each Saturday night. She had spent $5 on lottery tickets in the belief that she was undoubtedly going to be a winner. Nothing would screw up her plans quite as much as suddenly being a millionaire and having so much to lose. It was on this basis that she simply assumed that she would win on the Saturday prior to the opening of the Electronika show. She was a firm believer in the rule which states that whatever can go wrong will go wrong and at the most inconvenient time. In fact, she planned to put that rule to her very great advantage in wreaking vengeance against the Electronika Internationale Trade Show.

Samantha turned to page two of the newspaper where the lottery numbers would be printed only to find that they were still showing the previous week's winners.

She would just have to buy another newspaper later that night or in the morning. Inasmuch as she had paid for it, she was browsing through the newspaper when she decided, for reasons that she could never have thought of, to take a look at the business section. The anger within her rose to a fever pitch when she saw the lead story on the front page of the business section. The headline screamed, "Electronika to Bring 100,000 Visitors to Town." There was a file photo of some fancy exhibits from a previous show with a crowd mingled around them and a story which continued on to the inside pages detailing the history of this giant electronics show and its value to the city.

"Damn," she cursed herself silently. Not one word about her threat to the show. But how could there be? Certainly the Expo Center wasn't going to call in the newspaper. That would be equivalent of a ship captain drilling a large hole in the bottom of his hull to let the water out. She wanted the publicity to start appearing. It looked as if Samantha would have to organize her own publicity campaign. She set about doing just that.

Nobody looked twice at the woman using the coin phone near the university library. Even in the wee hours of the morning it was not unusual to see people making calls to anywhere in the world and even hooking up fax machines or modems to these telephones to transmit their data or messages. One call to the newspaper's switchboard, which was manned 24 hours a day, got her the fax number to the managing editor's office. The Public

Library was, of course, closed in the middle of the night. But universities could always be relied on to be open late, if not 24 hours a day, and to have computers available for those who needed them. Samantha sought out a bank of computers and selected one which was connected to a nine pin dot matrix printer. She typed in a test line and sent it to the printer to make certain it would come out dark enough for fax transmission. Satisfied that this would be an acceptable way to generate the messages, she organized one for the newspaper editor and then with a smile on her face tapped out a short message she would send to Harry this night. About 6 a.m. on Sunday morning, Darryl's call roused Harry from a deep sleep.

"Howdy, pal! My boys intercepted a fax transmission to the machine in Carly's office about 3 a.m. this morning. Do you want me to read it to you?"

Harry swung his feet off of the bed and sat upright holding the phone to his ear. "Sure, go ahead."

"Dear Harry, don't worry about going to church this morning. You're fucked. Not even God is going to be able to pull you out of this one. Love, Sam."

"Oh, sweet Jesus, isn't that wonderful. Just what I need to start my day." Harry was now standing up. His face was turning beet red as the rage within him swelled. "This son of a bitch is just jerking my chain. This has gone far enough."

Darryl's voice came through the phone. "This time we know where the sending station is."

"Fantastic," screamed Harry. "Let's move on it."

"Not so fast," said Darryl. "The sending station turns out to be a coin operated fax machine at the airport."

"I don't give a God damn if it was in the Vatican City. Somebody had to have seen who sent the fax." Harry continued, "Let's find out who owns that concession and get them to cough up the charge card number that was used to send the fax."

Darryl was way ahead of him. "My guys have already done that. Whoever sent the fax paid for it by feeding dollar bills into the slot. We have retrieved all of the currency that was in the machine and there were only two $1 bills. They had to come from whoever sent the fax. I have sent the currency over to the lab to print the stuff for us."

Harry was elated. "That's great, we got him." His elation soon withered as Darryl continued. "Well, there is where the problem starts Harry. The lab guys have used three different techniques on the bills and the problem is that they got so many prints on them, they got so much DNA all over them, they wouldn't have any idea what belongs to anyone. The prints were useless and even if we could lift a DNA spot, you got to have a suspect who you can use for an exemplar to match up against it. That is what we ain't got."

"Well what about the sender? Somebody had to have seen him."

"Yeah, you would think so except the shift changed there at 4 a.m. All the people who were on at 3 o'clock have all gone home and we have contacted a couple of them but nobody saw nothing. The fax machine is over by the bank of coin phones in the arrivals lounge and since there were no planes coming into that concourse in the wee hours of the morning, there was nobody working out there. Whoever used this fax went to a concourse that they knew would be deserted, found the machine and sent the fax where nobody could observe him doing it. Look, I'm not saying that it's a complete dead end. There's nothing here to go on yet, but we're going to continue to push. At least we now know how one of these faxes was sent and where it was sent from."

"Hey, what about the video cameras in the terminal? Maybe they caught this guy." Harry was reaching. Hoping against hope that this might be the lead that would nab his perpetrator.

"Been there, done that," replied Darryl. "It seems that the TV cameras are set up to shoot down the hallway of the terminal and they don't shoot into these little alcoves where the telephones and fax machines are. In fact, since the terminal was mostly shut down and was on half lighting, they got one image of some little guy who walked down a hall, ducked into the men's room, must have taken a leak, came out, walked back toward the cameras, went into the phone area, must have made a phone call, and then left. When he was walking back toward the camera, the light was so low we can't even resolve an image. All I can tell you about the guy is that he's short. If you ask me, this is not the guy we're looking for. Who we're looking for must have slid in there somehow without being observed by the camera."

"Balls! Don't tell me that we can't get anything done with that videotape. Let's send it to the Feds and ask them to enhance it."

"That's what I like about you, Harry, you're such a deep thinker. I think I'm going to do just what you said. You know Brice Youngmann over at the Feebies?"

"No, I've heard of him. I think I've seen his name in some articles but I never met the guy," replied Harry.

"They're the only ones I know that have the equipment to enhance these images. It's the kind of thing they do when they're trying to get a make on bank robbers so we're going to give him a call in a little while. I don't want to wake him up at this hour. Hopefully they'll say yes and we can ship this video up to them tonight and their whiz kids will take a look at it tomorrow. You know that they usually don't work weekends in the lab up there."

Harry was beginning to perspire. "I'm really getting unhappy about this whole thing. What do you think? Where do we go from here?"

"Well, I'm kinda wondering Harry, this guy talks about you going to church. Maybe we ought to put a watch not only on your house but on the church that you normally go to. Let's see if we can get a make on somebody whose hanging around trying to eyeball you. What do you think about that?"

"Yeah, that would be real neat except for one thing, Darryl. I'm strictly a Christmas and Easter customer at the church. In fact, I think if I walked in there on an off week they would think that the world was coming to an end. I'm not exactly the ultra-religious type."

"Shit. Anymore bad news?" sighed Darryl.

"Naw"

"Well, there is one other thing that you ought to know about. When my guy called me at the beginning of the watch this morning, he told me that there was also a routine signal from the Feds that the Vice President may be coming to town to deliver the keynote speech at this grand hoop-di-doo in your pleasure palace. That means, among other things, that we got to fill them in on this potential threat to His Excellency. We got to copy them with all of these faxes and phone calls or whatever, whenever they come into us. You know it's routine and it really isn't anything for us to be overly concerned about because they take care of protecting their own. But, we would look like first class schmucks if we knew something that we didn't tell them about and the Vice President got inconvenienced or, like maybe even dead."

By this time, Harry had taken the cordless phone with him to the kitchen. He had poured a cup of cold coffee from the pot and stuck it into the microwave to try and revive it. Hearing this last piece of news, he slumped into the booth of the dinette in the kitchen and just stared blankly at the rose printed wallpaper with his eyes focused about two feet behind the wall.

"Harry, Harry, you there?"

"Yeah, I guess I'm here, this is not exactly what I need. Is there some way we can discourage this guy from coming down here?"

"Well, Harry, I'd assume that if the Feds think that their boy may be in trouble, that they in turn will discourage him from coming down here so that we don't have to. In fact, just us peasants have no way at all of getting any input to the White House or to the Office of the Vice President, so it has to be the Feds. On the other hand, what I'm concerned about for you, old pal, is if it gets to the press that the Vice President cancels a visit to Electronika because of security risks, what's that going to do for people who are coming to go to the show who may be concerned about their personal safety?"

"Interesting question, Darryl."

"You bet your ass it's interesting. If he comes here and he gets blown up, you look like shit. If he doesn't come because you can't guarantee his safety, guess what? You still look like shit. My suggestion is it's better to look like shit and have the Vice President alive. What do you think?"

A long pause. "Yeah, you know it is. Let's turn over everything we got to them. Then if anything goes wrong, maybe we can cop out on the basis that the Feds co-opted all of our options."

"I love it, Harry. Jesus, you are one devious son of a bitch. It's no wonder I love you. Don't sweat it, I'm going to take care of everything. I'll call you back later this afternoon. Say a little prayer for me, too, pal." Darryl hung up. Harry pressed the button on the cordless phone to disconnect it and swilled back a mouthful of semi-warm, unsweetened, three-day old coffee. The day was not starting off well.

8

The general manager of Electronika Internationale was Albert A. Atkinson. Albert, (a/k/a AAA) was not only the general manager of the show, but owned 25% of the show. He used to own 100% of it, but a couple of years before he had sold off a majority interest in the show to Expo Holdings Internationale, an overseas investment company, for more millions of dollars than he thought he could ever live to spend or use.

The sun had come up early in the gulf stream and he was aboard the yacht Lektronic when his first mate knocked persistently on the cabin door. "All right, for Christ's sake, come on in," yelled Albert Atkinson.

A crisp "Aye, Sir" and the door opened. A deeply tanned young man dressed all in white with the insignia of the yacht emblazoned on the left pocket of his shirt handed an envelope to Albert Atkinson. "This signal came in for you just a minute ago Sir, it seemed urgent." The steward handed the envelope to Albert Atkinson and retreated as he had entered.

AAA sat up in bed and ripped open the envelope. The message was straight forward and did not leave room for negotiation. It simply said, "Received telephone communication at 0652 hours. Caller identified himself as Brice Youngmann, special agent in charge, Federal Bureau of Investigation, New York City. Mr. Youngmann insists that we put in to the nearest port and

70

that you contact him by land line at this telephone number. We are to respond immediately and we are to call back within 15 minutes advising that we are complying and indicating when we expect to make land."

Albert Atkinson reached for the intercom telephone and rang the bridge of the yacht Lektronic. Captain Murphy answered the phone. "Aye, Sir, good morning to you. How can I serve you?"

"Hey Murph, do you know anything about a phone call supposedly coming from an FBI guy? I just got the message handed to me."

"Yes Sir, Mr. Atkinson. It was me who took the call and I wrote it down. It sounded legit to me. That's all I can tell you."

"Well, what have we done? Did you change our course to head back to land?"

"Negative, Sir," replied Captain Murphy. "You are in command of this vessel Sir, not the FBI. I'm taking her where you tell me."

Albert Atkinson felt great personal pride in the attitude of Captain Murphy and in knowing that he, in fact, was more important than the federal agency to this weathered gentleman of the seas.

"Thanks, Captain, but I think under the circumstances we'd better take this seriously. What's our position and can you calculate a course for me?"

"Aye Sir, I can and I have. We can come around to a bearing of 273 and at average cruising speed I make that we should be able to put into Fort Lauderdale in about four hours."

"Can we do it any faster?"

"Aye Sir, if we go to full speed, we certainly can shave that by at least 35 or 40 minutes but we will use a hell of a lot of fuel to do it."

"Do we have enough fuel on board to run it full speed?"

"Yes Sir, we do," replied Captain Murphy.

"O.K., Murph, Fort Lauderdale it is. Call into Pier 66, give them our ETA, tell them we want an accommodation with no publicity and that you have no passengers on board. I don't even want them to know I'm with you. Then call this guy back on the marine phone and give him our ETA. I'll be ready for breakfast in about 30 minutes on the aft deck and we will try to figure out what the hell is going on here."

It was only 6:30 pacific time in Las Vegas when the telephone rang at the hotel. Carlton Bentwood, III was ensconced in an oversized and overpriced suite of rooms on the top floor of the chic hostelry when the telephone rang and the smarmy voice of the hall porter cum concierge came through. "Bon jour, Monsieur Bentwood. This is Marcel, the concierge. I have a matter of utmost urgency and delicacy to convey to you Monsieur. May I be so bold as to come to your rooms at this time?"

Carly had known this "concierge" for many years and knew that he was as phony as a $3 bill. Just what this matter of the utmost urgency and delicacy could be quite eluded him but in his stupor all he could think to say was, "Sure, come on right now."

A few minutes later, a polite, quiet knock came at the door and Carly admitted his sycophantic concierge. The concierge seemed to be disturbed as he explained to Monsieur Bentwood that the hotel had received a call just a moment or two ago from the head of the Federal Bureau of Investigation at New York, insisting that he be put through to Mr. Bentwood immediately. This individual would not accept that Mr. Bentwood couldn't be disturbed. "In fact Monsieur Bentwood, this rude individual went so far as to say that if I did not get my ass up to your room and give you this message within 10 minutes, that he would have me deported. He obviously does not know that I was born in New Orleans. But I do not care to have a problem with the authorities and I don't know what kind of a problem Monsieur Bentwood may have, but I suggest that perhaps a response to his telephone call may be in order. No?"

"Yeah, sure, thanks Marcel, you did well." Carly held the door aside for the concierge to leave. Marcel hesitated ever so slightly in the expectation that perhaps a gratuity might be forthcoming and with the failure of such to materialize made a half bow and exited stage left. Eileen called from the bedroom in her syrupy southern accent. "What's going on Carly, honey?"

"Nothing Sugar Pie, y'all just lie back there and grab a few more Z's while old Carly takes care of a little business, heah?" Carly quietly pulled the door from the bedroom to the salon closed and went to the telephone on the Louis XIV desk. Sullenly, he dialed the access code for an outside long distance line followed by the ten digits in the message from Marcel.

"This is Youngmann, who is this?" was the response. "My name is Carlton Bentwood, III," started Carly when he was interrupted by the FBI agent.

"Thank you for calling. I know who you are. Please listen carefully to me because I have some information that is extremely important. My first question to you I want you to answer yes or no. Can your conversation with me be overheard by any third party as far as you know?"

"No, I'm alone."

"Do you have any reason to believe that any third party can pick up an extension and overhear this call?"

"Well, I don't know how the telephone switchboard works in the hotel but I can tell you Mr. Youngmann that I am here by myself. My wife is in the adjoining room sound asleep. She has a telephone next to the bed, but I'm assuming if she picked it up I would hear it. What is all this secrecy about?"

The color started to drain from Carly's face like one of those oil and water desk toys that changes color slowly when you flip it over. He was listening as this unknown voice at the end of the phone explained that the Vice President of the United States was probably going to show up at the Electronika show and that they had reason to believe that a bomber was going to show up at the show as well. Carly listened in silence. When the FBI agent had completed his statement, he inquired whether or not Carlton Bentwood, III was aware of any threats to the facility.

"Well, yes, we did get a fax from some unknown individual and I turned it over to Chief Mills, of our security department. I'm quite certain that it is in very capable hands. I have no reason to have any concern about it."

"You left it in Harry Mills' hands and you have no concern?" asked the FBI man. "Mr. Bentwood, when are you coming back to the city?"

"Well, Eileen and I should be coming back on Tuesday," replied the now shaken Carly.

"May I respectfully suggest to you, Sir, that that may be a little bit too late. It is now about 9:30 here. May I suggest to you that you get the noon flight back and we'll have a car meet you at the airport. You will find a reservation has been made for you on Flight 431 which leaves Vegas at 12:05 p.m." The phone went dead. Clearly, Carlton Bentwood, III wasn't used to being treated in this manner. People did not tell him to take a specific flight and people did not go and make the reservations for

75

him without his consent. He didn't even know if the reservations were first class and he certainly had no intention of flying economy. But he was shaken and he had no alternative but to do as he was told.

Carly picked up the phone again and pressed the buttons for room service. "This is Mr. Bentwood in Penthouse 3. Would y'all please send up breakfast for two, fresh *croissants, confiture, café au lait*, and some scrambled eggs with grits." Carlton had used up as much of the french language as he knew in ordering the first three items, but hadn't a clue how one might say scrambled eggs or grits *en Francais*. He opened the door to the bedroom to find Eileen sitting half upright in bed. She had on a beautiful powder blue negligee and her arms extended to him inviting him to join her in the bed. "What's the matter Sugar Honey? You look just awful."

"You bet your ass I look awful. We're going to have to leave here Honey. We got to go back to New York today so y'all better get your sweet cheeks out of that bed and start getting that hairdo of yours fixed up and that face put on. I done ordered us a mess of breakfast and we gonna get going."

"But Sugar, y'all promised to take me to the casino today." She was beginning to whine.

Carly, who was shaken by the call and who was now annoyed at having to deal with his wife's lack of perception as to the gravity of the situation, picked up a straight back chair, carried it to the bed and set it down by the side of the bed in the style of a doctor attending a young patient. He took Eileen's hands in his, looked her in

76

the eyes and explained to her the nature of the phone call. All she could say repeatedly was, "Shit Honey." When he got through, he turned to Eileen and he said, "Yes honey, shit indeed, now get them sweet cheeks of yours the hell out of the sack and into that shower. O.K., Sweetie?"

It was 8:45 when Harry pulled into the reserved parking lot behind the Expo Center and let himself into the darkened building. He knew that none of his normal security patrols would enter the executive suite and check the messages on the fax machine because that wasn't their normal beat. Yet nothing that was normal had happened in the previous two days. Therefore, to be on the safe side, he better go get the message off the machine before that fat ass big mouth Tabatha got her hands on it. Harry waved himself past the security guard near the loading dock and walked straight into the facility. He ran up the non-moving escalator stairs until he reached the uppermost level where the executive office was ensconced. Harry let himself in quickly and went to the fax machine. He found the original message which had been intercepted by Darryl's spooks. The message was exactly as Darryl had read it to him. Harry activated the fax machine to see if it had any further information as to the sending station, but it had none whatsoever. He activated the printout feature on the machine to print out the incoming log. That prevented somebody coming behind him and retrieving any information as to faxes which may have come in since the previous printout. As he turned to leave the office, the telephone on the private line of Carly Bentwood was ringing off the hook. Without knowing why, Harry picked the phone up and said, "Hello." He would probably never do such a rash act again.

"Who is this?" demanded the caller.

"This is Harry Mills, Chief of Security, Midtown Expo Center, you are reaching a private line Sir, whoever you are, you've got a wrong number."

"The hell I have Harry. Then it's true, isn't it?" asked the caller.

"Who is this, do I know you?"

"No you don't know me, Harry. It's Mark Bates. I'm the assistant managing editor at The Ledger and I guess you just confirmed the rumor."

"Well excuse me, Mr. Bates, whoever you are. I don't know what rumor you're talking about, and I didn't confirm a Goddamn thing. If you print it I'm going to sue your ass."

"Well if you don't know anything about it Chief, then why would you be so concerned about whether I print it or not and tell me what you'rel doing there on a Sunday morning at 8:55? Anyhow, it's really Carlton Bentwood that I want to talk with. Can you tell me how I can find him?"

"No Sir, I cannot comment on the whereabouts of Mr. Bentwood and as to why I am in the office on a

Sunday morning, I'm the Chief of Security of this facility as you are well aware and I don't believe that it makes any difference as to why I'm here, nor do I have any intention of responding further to your question."

"Oh, I see. No intention of commenting further. Then after the building blows up, may I call you for a comment or should we just should forget about it, Sir?"

Harry's heart beat faster and a wave of nausea came over him. "Now wait a minute, what are you talking about and where did you get the information?"

"I don't have any problem in being candid with you and I wish you could be candid with me and trust me. My chief got a fax from somebody named Sam telling them to check into the bomb threat against the Electronika show. He also handed me another note saying that our Washington bureau advised us that there was a possibility that the Vice President was going to be here for the show also. I mean it's very obviously a story and we have to follow it up. Your reaction tells me that in fact it is true and that you do know something about a threat against the show so I'd like to meet with you. I'd like to know what you're doing about it. This is a big story, Chief. I can't sit on it because there is just no way to cover up something like this. How about if I come over there now and we have a cup of coffee?"

"No, that's absolutely impossible but give me your name again and phone number." Harry grabbed a piece of paper off of Tabatha's desk and wrestled the pen from his shirt pocket. He wrote Mr. Bates' telephone number down and promised that he would return a call to him within the hour.

Things were not only going from bad to worse, but they were getting there a hell of a lot faster than Harry could have imagined.

Aboard the yacht Lektronic, Albert A. Atkinson held the microphone in his hand as he called the south Florida marine operator and passed to her the number for Mr. Youngmann. Atkinson was connected in just a few seconds and after introductions from one to the other, he asked, "I have complied with your request, Sir. My captain has put us on a bearing for Fort Lauderdale and we should be in by noon time. Now, Sir, can you give me some indication as to the nature of this emergency?"

"I respectfully suggest to you, Sir, that I am not at liberty to provide that information over a radio telephone link. I can only suggest to you that this is a matter of the greatest urgency and importance both to your commercial enterprise and to the national interests of the United States of America."

Atkinson was stunned. He had no idea what was going on and inasmuch as he was totally apolitical, couldn't conceive of how anything in his business could have any impact whatsoever upon the interest of the United States other than the outrageous amount of taxes which he forked over each year. "Very well Mr. Youngmann, as soon as we arrive in port I shall find a telephone and call you back. You can expect to hear from me before 1 p.m.

today."

Youngmann replied, "Mr. Atkinson, I appreciate your cooperation. I can assure you that we have not asked you to change your plans based on conjecture or whim. I would ask you one thing further, Sir. Please place the call from a public coin phone where you won't be overheard by others."

Atkinson replied with a simple, "Will do," and terminated the conversation.

It was 9:28 a.m. when the security guard at the Expo Center opened the public address system and intoned, "Chief Mills, you have a visitor at main security. Chief Mills, you have a visitor at main security."

Harry hadn't been expecting anyone and was kind of annoyed that anyone should be presumptuous enough to assume that he was in the facility on a Sunday morning. He picked up the nearest wall telephone and punched in the number for the security desk. "Who the hell is looking for me?"

"Sorry, Sir. There is a Mark Bates here from The Ledger. He said that you asked him to come right over." Harry realized his dilemma in an instant. Bates was obviously sitting in the steel straight-backed chair at the security office and could hear one side of the conversation from that office. He knew that Mills was in fact in the facility. He also knew that Mills was aware that Mark Bates was also there. Harry would like to duck any interview or confrontation but there was no way which he could envision to avoid seeing this guy.

"O.K., ask Mr. Bates to wait with you and I will come down."

A few minutes later, Harry collected the eager Mark Bates and escorted him to a sitting area in the main lobby of the facility. The building was deserted except for the two of them and a couple of security workers. Bates spoke first. "What additional security measures has the Center taken to ensure against this terrorist?"

Harry regarded Bates and said, "You know, I'm not certain how I can answer you. I'm not sure what you are talking about, Sir, and if you would be kind enough to fill me in then perhaps I could respond to you in a cogent manner."

Bates clearly realized that Harry was stalling for time and probing for information. What the hell, might as well tell him what I know and see what I can suck out of him. "Mr. Mills, we know that a threat has been made to disrupt the Electronika Internationale exhibition opening this week. We also know that the Vice President of the United States is likely to be at this meeting to address it."

"So what do you want me to do about it? I'm not sure what this is all about, still."

"Well let me add one more bit of background

for you, Sir. People have a way of confirming things by the way that they either deny or fail to respond to questions and after 30 years in the news business, I have a pretty good nose for when nerves are on edge. Just like I can tell you frankly that you are telling me by your body language and by your demeanor that I am absolutely correct in what I'm suggesting to you. But let me tell you that we placed calls to quite a few contacts in various federal, state and local police agencies and in almost every instance I was met with the sort of response which confirmed by denial everything which I asked. I have nobody on record. I have no other evidence, but I can tell you that I am 100% certain that I know what I'm talking about and I'm watching you while I'm talking to you and you're telling me that I am right on target. So what do you say we both stop the bullshit and you let me try to help you."

Mills thought it was a neat speech but he also had a natural distrust of the press. He knew that all a reporter was interested in was selling newspapers and grabbing that transient few moments of byline celebrity for himself which a story would generate. Controversy and tragedy are the stock in trade of the media. Mills had known for many years that there was no such thing as a friend in the media. It didn't make any difference whether they were newspaper, radio or TV, they were all the same punch of piranha just looking to feed on the misery of the human condition.

"Well, I don't think I can help you Mr. Bates. I really don't know much about any of this and if you have some information that you would like to present to me, I'd be glad to take it into consideration."

Mark Bates leaned forward in his chair and spoke quietly into Harry's ear with his mouth about six inches from Harry's face. His bad breath was almost as offensive as his bad taste. Bates quietly told him, "Mr. Mills, I'm going with this story in the morning edition. You have confirmed everything I want to know and I intend to add one more sentence which is that Chief Harry Mills of the Midtown Expo Center was unable to confirm that any additional security measures had been initiated to protect the well being of the Vice President of our country. I hope you enjoy reading it."

"You run a story like that and I believe that you may find yourself in court." It was a hollow threat and as Harry spoke the words he realized how ridiculous he sounded.

"That may be, Sir. But I warrant that you will find yourself in much deeper shit before this is over. Have a nice day. Call me when you want to talk." Bates thrust his card into Harry's hand and turned to walk out.

"Hang on a minute, Bates. Maybe we can talk, strictly on background, understood?"

"Absolutely, are you ready to talk now?" asked Bates, who was still walking toward the door. Harry caught up to him and took him by the elbow.

"Look, you know I'm the head of security here. I don't run the damn show. We have other people to consider. I cannot talk to you until I have talked to Bentwood and/or Atkinson. I will try to get in touch with them and get back to you today."

84

"That's fine Chief. I appreciate your willingness to help. We got to go to press at 7 o'clock tonight. Do you think perhaps you can get to me before then?"

"I'll be back to you by 5 p.m. this afternoon. I'll ring the beeper number that's on this card, O.K.?"

"Yeah, that's fine. I will look forward to hearing from you."

With that, Harry held open the door for Bates and ushered him out of the facility.

As soon as Bates had left, Harry retreated to his own office, closed the door and went directly to his desk. He picked up the phone and quickly dialed the digits to Darryl Jones' beeper. He entered his own private telephone number and sat there drumming his fingers on the desk for what seemed an interminable amount of time. It wasn't very long before Darryl returned his call.

"What's up, big guy?" asked Darryl.

"We got problems buddy. This thing is getting worse. I had some reporter or editor from a newspaper here by the name of Bates who seems to know all about the threat against the Electronika show. He is either going to run the story tomorrow claiming that I confirmed the rumor or we've got to dissuade him somehow. I don't think he's going to listen to me. Can you help me put a muzzle on this guy?"

"Jesus, Harry, I don't know how we are going to shut this guy up. You know how they are when they smell a story. About the only way you can shut them up is when it's the life of a kid that's in jeopardy right then and there. Does he know about the Vice President?"

"Yeah, he seems to know about everything and I wonder where he's getting the information." Harry's statement was more a rhetorical question. He assumed that the information was coming from somebody in one of the police agencies who was just repaying a favor to the guy in the newspaper.

Darryl answered, "I can tell you where he's getting the information. He's getting it from Sam. He's already called the guys at the State, ATF, FBI, Highway Patrol and NYPD. In fact, Chief Barrow is over at the PD and is pissed off because she didn't know anything about this and claims that we were trying to keep her in the dark. The bitch is screaming bloody murder, yelling that this is her turf and her beat and she wants to be in the loop."

"Well for Christ's sake, I don't know what we are going to do at this point. I guess we are just going to have to let the newspaper do what it wants and I'm going to have to go ahead and do whatever I gotta do to protect this fucking show and that Vice President of ours." Harry's mood was changing from one of bedevilment into absolute resolve. He was going to stop this threat no matter what he had to do. His only problem was that he didn't have a clue as to what he might do.

Darryl's voice came back on the line. "Here's the situation as of this minute, Harry. Some guy by the name of Atkinson, who is the president of the trade show, is out on his yacht off of Fort Lauderdale. The Feds have got him heading for shore and they are going to clue him into the situation when he gets to a telephone. They found your boss stashed in some poncey little hotel in Las Vegas and they are getting him on a plane which will be back here late this afternoon. The intention is that we will have a meeting at Youngmann's office at 6 p.m. It will be a representative from each one of the federal and state agencies and your good self. In order to mollify our lady chief of police, she has been invited, too, although most of the guys don't really trust her a whole hell of a lot."

"O.K., where did you say the meeting was going to be?"

"Six p.m. at Youngmann's office in the Fed Building. Just tell them that you're there to see him and your name will be on a list at the door. Keep your beeper with you and if there is any change, I will be in touch with you."

Harry asked, "Yeah, but in the meantime, what do I say to this schmuck from the newspaper?"

"Well, I can't tell you what to say. I can only give you the same advice my father gave me before I got married. He told me to keep my mouth shut."

"Yeah." Harry had no cards to play in this game. "See you at 6, OK?"

Chief Harry Mills replaced the telephone receiver and sat at his desk as he continued to doodle on his pad. He knew there were two more calls that he would have to make. He had to call his old lady and bring her up to date. Something inside him told him to get in touch with his own attorney to make sure that his will was in order.

❾

Samantha slept late Sunday morning. Saturday had been a big day and her tests had gone well. She knew that Harry must be going nuts by this time and she ensured that he couldn't keep a cover on this by sending a fax off to the managing editor of the newspaper. Surely, they could be relied upon to hop on this story. About 11 o'clock she drew a bath and languorously immersed herself in a sea of aromatic suds. As she lay with her head against a rolled up towel at the back of the tub, she thought to herself that she must be the only terrorist in the entire world who prepared to fight the good fight by taking a long, sensual, warm bath.

In order that her life be as normal as possible, Samantha thought that this would be a perfect day to call one of the men whom she sometimes dated and arrange for a Sunday afternoon lunch and maybe an afternoon of sex and fun at her apartment. Samantha dried herself off and wrapped her hair in a towel before pulling the chain on the drain to let the water escape her bath. She started to find out if she could set up a date before she picked out her clothes for the day and called up the guy who was her first choice for that afternoon. As luck would have it, he was very flattered to hear from her and agreed to meet her at a local yuppie beanery for lunch at 1 o'clock.

Samantha made certain he understood that she intended to make an afternoon of it but had some other plans for the evening. In order not to injure his male ego, Samantha left the impression that she had to be with an old aunt that evening and that it was a family obligation which she must honor. The guy readily agreed to the luncheon date. Samantha picked out the clothes which she thought would be a turn on for the guy and got dressed for a casual Sunday afternoon rendezvous.

"Oh Harry," she thought. "Don't you wish you could relax this way, too?"

It was 10:47 when the telephone rang in Carly's suite of rooms. His wife had just finished packing her clothes and throwing his into a matching Louis Vuitton suitcase. It was his smarmy concierge friend on the phone. "A Mr. Nelson from the FBI is here to see you. He's on his way up, Sir."

"Thanks. I'll let him in." A few minutes later the knock came at the door of the Bentwood suite and Carlton Bentwood, III admitted George Nelson, a special agent of the Federal Bureau of Investigation.

"Good morning Mr. Bentwood. I have been asked to take you and Mrs. Bentwood to the airport." As he was speaking, Nelson held out his FBI credentials for Bentwood's review.

"But what about my car, I have a rented car?"

"That's all taken care of Sir. If I may have the keys, I have an assistant downstairs who will return the car to the agency for you and we will take you in an official car."

"You know, I don't like this a damn bit. Am I under arrest or something?" Bentwood was getting agitated.

"Not at all, Sir. Mr. Youngmann did not know that you had a rented car. He felt that rather than have you go in a taxi that we should extend the courtesy of the government to you and deliver you and your wife to the VIP lounge at the airline."

Hearing those magic words "VIP lounge," Bentwood felt more at ease and decided that he could endure being a celebrity for awhile. By 11:15, the FBI agent with a driver and the Bentwoods as passengers had headed out to the airport. Within 10 minutes the car pulled around to the back side of the terminal building. The Bentwoods were escorted into an elevator that took them to the second level and an interior passageway that connected to a special VIP lounge. Nelson advised them, "Your baggage is being checked on the flight for you Sir and here are the tickets and boarding passes for you and Mrs. Bentwood."

Carly took the tickets from the agent, and as he was opening the ticket envelope to see check the class of service, the agent spoke again saying, "You will note that they are assigned in first class section, Sir."

This is more like it, thought Carly. "Thank you. That is very considerate."

A black gentlemen of a great number of years in a white waiter's jacket approached the trio who were the only passengers in the VIP room. "May I bring y'all something to drink or a cup of coffee?" asked the steward whose name badge proclaimed him to be Ozzie.

Mrs. Bentwood spoke immediately saying, "I believe that I will have a Dewar's and water if y'all please." She was really hooked on that phony southern drawl. Carly looked at Ozzie and said, "Just make mine Jack Daniels straight up and I guess you maybe ought to make it a double, OK?" The waiter nodded, "Yassir. And you suh?"

The FBI agent simply required a coffee and some crackers if they had any.

They sat in silence for a few minutes until the waiter reappeared with the drinks. As he drew away, the Bentwoods raised their glasses to clink them together. They caught the agent looking at them as though they were some sort of specimens in a petri dish. Indeed, the agent was thinking to himself that these have to be two of the most superficial assholes he had ever met in his entire career of dealing with superficial assholes.

Carly repeatedly pumped the agent for information as to what this emergency was all about. But all he could get from Mr. Nelson was that he was simply doing an errand at the request of the special agent in charge from New York. He was certain all would be made clear upon their arrival there. The only thing the agent could tell Mr. and Mrs. Bentwood was that they would be met at the plane by another agent who would escort them to a high level top security meeting in Manhattan.

"The one thing I have been asked to advise you is that Agent Youngmann requests that you do not make any telephone calls or relate any information to third parties until you have had an opportunity to be completely briefed by him and others who will attend this meeting."

Ozzie answered the muted ring of the telephone behind the bar, simply said, "Thank you," and hung up. He shuffled over to the three waiting VIP's and said, "The flight is ready for boarding folks."

Now mollified that he would be flying first class, and strengthened by his first drink of the day, Carly was quite at ease as he fished a $5 bill out of his pocket and left it on the coffee table for Ozzie. They were on their way down the hall to board the flight.

It was a little before 12 when the yacht Lektronic slid through the Port Everglades cut and swung north to the marina. Atkinson felt the engines stop. The yacht had to lay-to for a few minutes before the bridge would be fully opened. He heard the signal of the ship's horn and knew that they would be dockside in a few minutes. He had dressed in a pair of chinos and a short sleeved chino shirt with a web belt and a pair of deck shoes with white socks. Atkinson's intention was to look like one of the hired hands when he got off the ship and sought out the pay phone. All of the time that the vessel had been making for Fort Lauderdale, he kept thinking about what this could be that required this drastic action on his part. He felt he had to comply, however. If the matter were as urgent as Agent Youngmann seemed to indicate, then he wanted to discharge his obligations as a good citizen. If, on the other hand, in his opinion Youngmann was acting out a lie, he had enough friends in high places in Washington to ensure that this agent would find himself policing an Indian reservation in North Dakota for the rest of his career.

Carly probably wasn't the only one who felt in need of a drink to fortify himself that Sunday morning. Chief Harry Mills looked at his watch and noted that it was just about noontime. That meant he could have his first drink of the day as well. He always thought that the laws which prohibited the sale of liquor before noon on Sunday were somewhat asinine. The theory was that if alcohol were not available, more people would be inclined to attend church. His experience as a police officer for many years led him to conclude that those who were bound for church on Sunday were hardly going to stop by to snort a short one on the way. Those who were more inclined to Absolut than to absolution were certainly not going to head for the church rather than the bar unless they could nip into the sacramental wine before the Padre got there.

Harry sought out a nearby hotel which featured a large Sunday buffet. It included all of the champagne or mimosas that you could drink along with your fill of smoked fish, fruit, bagels and rolls, roasts, desserts, and 57 different types of salads. The other outstanding feature of this particular buffet was that the management afforded to Harry the same courtesy discount which he would have enjoyed as a still working member of the local constabulary. By the time he had destroyed his fourth piece of roast beef and quaffed his fifth glass of cheap champagne, Harry thought he might slow down a bit before he impaired his ability to reason at this afternoon's meeting.

He asked for the check, calculated the tip based on 10% of the discounted amount which he anticipated paying, and left the money for the waiter on the table. Harry settled his tab, and left the hotel for a brisk walk around downtown while he tried to clear his headache and focus his thoughts for the afternoon.

A few miles away in a yuppie area of town, Samantha and her date settled into a couple of plastic chairs on the deck of one of the local bistros. She had ordered her favorite of fettuccine *tre colore* and a glass of zinfandel. Her date had opted for the pasta *putanesca* and he preferred Soave. While waiting for their orders, they had destroyed a copious amount of foccacio which they had dipped into an admixture of grated cheese and extra virgin olive oil. Samantha, who knew that putanesca meant *in the style of a whore*, thought it especially appropriate considering what she had in mind for the balance of her week. Perhaps her young man understood also that it reflected his thoughts for the afternoon. In fact, they joked about carbing up for strenuous activities that afternoon.

After lunch, Samantha and Bernie would stroll the neighborhood, visit one of the bookstores and browse through the books on theater and art. By 3 o'clock she would have him back at her apartment and fuck his brains out until 6 o'clock when she needed to get rid of him.

To the casual observer they were just another pair of yuppies in their late 20's or early 30's doing their thing on a lovely Sunday afternoon.

More than a thousand miles south of New York, Atkinson sought out a coin phone on the lower level of the Pier 66 marina. He had stopped at the cashier's desk and bought $10 worth of quarters. He didn't want to place this call on his credit card which would leave a billing record.

When the operator advised him to deposit several dollars in coins, he fed the quarters in until he had satisfied the machine and was connected directly to Brice Youngmann. Youngmann asked if he were calling from a coin phone and when Atkinson said that he was, Youngmann took down the number and asked him to please hang up and wait for the telephone to ring. Before doing so, Youngmann asked if he knew whether or not that particular phone could accept incoming calls. Atkinson had no idea and so Youngmann advised him to check his watch and if he did not hear the phone ring within two minutes exactly, to please replace the call again. Atkinson did as he was requested.

In less than 30 seconds the coin box phone started to ring and he picked it up to find Youngmann on the other end. After exchanging pleasantries, Youngmann advised Atkinson that he had a matter of great urgency to relate that would take him a couple of minutes to detail. Youngmann wished not to be interrupted and at the conclusion of his statement he would ask Mr. Atkinson to undertake some action at the request of the government. Atkinson agreed to stand by quietly and listen to Youngmann's exposition.

In a very matter of fact tone, Youngmann told

Atkinson exactly what he knew and left very little out particularly pointing out that the life of the Vice President of the United States could very well be in jeopardy. At the conclusion of his statement, Youngmann said, "Can we rely upon your discretion and your cooperation without hesitation?"

"Of course you can. What should I do?"

"I would like you to keep this telephone number with you, Sir." said Youngmann. "There is a meeting at my office in the federal building which will convene at 6 p.m. this afternoon. We very much would like to have you here if you can possibly make it. My assistants have checked the scheduled airlines and there is a flight from Fort Lauderdale at 2:15 which will have you at the airport here by 5 and we can have a car meet you."

Without hesitation Atkinson replied, "That won't be necessary. I will have our plane bring me up. It's at the Palm Beach airport. I will call now and have them come down to Fort Lauderdale and collect me. I can be there within four hours. As soon as I have arrangements made, my pilot or I will call you. It probably would help if you would send a car. We'll put in at Teterboro."

"Splendid. We really appreciate your cooperation in this matter, Sir." Youngmann then passed through to Atkinson two other phone numbers which he could use if the original one were busy. He would certainly have an agent meet him at Teterboro. Atkinson hung up and dialed up the beeper number for his pilot and punched in the number for the pay phone where he was standing. In less than 10 minutes the arrangements were made. The pilot should be landing at the general aviation section of the Fort Lauderdale International Airport in approximately 40 minutes. The plane had enough fuel on board to reach Teterboro, easily.

Back on board, Captain Murphy was told that Atkinson would be disembarking at this time. Murphy was to take the vessel back to Palm Beach to its home berth and, Atkinson specifically cautioned Murphy that he was to say absolutely nothing to anyone about the events of this day. When Atkinson could fill him in, he would tell him what he needed to know but he needed to rely on Murphy's obedience and discretion.

In less than 40 minutes a car delivered Atkinson to the north side of the airport where he could see the flag ship Lectra-I taxiing to the FBO terminal area. As the engines of the Gulfstream whined to a stop, the passenger gangway was thrown. Albert Atkinson immediately entered the aircraft. In less than another minute, the hatch was closed, the flight plan had been transmitted and Lectra-I was cleared for takeoff to north Jersey.

The Las Vegas flight pulled up to the terminal. As the first class passengers including Mr. and Mrs. Bentwood deplaned, two gentlemen in suits eyeballed the crowd coming off. One of the two suits approached Carly and said, "Mr. Bentwood?"

"Yes, I'm Carlton Bentwood."

"Would you and Mrs. Bentwood please come

98

with us? Your luggage will be collected and transported to your home for you. May I have your baggage checks, Sir?"

Carly handed over the baggage checks for the matched set of six pieces and was trying to advise the agent of his home address when the agent interrupted him. His luggage would arrive safely within the next hour or two.

Halfway down the terminal was an exit door that did not lead to the street level. The agents escorted the Bentwoods through this door and down a flight of stairs bringing them out onto the tarmac. A nondescript vehicle stood at the ready. One of the agents took the left side of the car while the other manned the right. Each held open one of the rear doors to permit the Bentwoods to seat themselves in the rear of the car. The agents took the seats in the front and drove off in the general direction of the cargo area.

"This is the treatment I should get all the time," thought Carly. He had seen many scenes like this in film but had never been afforded such treatment. It certainly beats rubbing shoulders with the great unwashed. Noting that they had ample time before the 6 p.m. meeting, the agents solicitously inquired if they might convey the Bentwoods to their home first so that Mrs. Bentwood may be more comfortable. It was clear that her presence at the meeting was neither required nor desired. The four rode in silence. At the Bentwood home the agents waited outside while Carly and Eileen went in and made some half-hearted excuse to the maid, explaining their arrival two days ahead of time.

Carly explained to the maid that there was some

mixup with the baggage and that the airline would be delivering it in a few hours. He, on the other hand, needed to simply freshen up because he had some associates waiting for him for an important business meeting. In a few minutes, Carly reappeared having changed his shirt, and splashed some expensive aftershave on his face. With the minimum of conversation, the agents left the walled subdivision in which the Bentwood manor stood and headed back south into the inner city and Carly Bentwood's appointment with destiny.

The flight from Fort Lauderdale landed without incident at 4:47 p.m. The pilot had radioed the ETA to the federal agents who had a car standing by at the airport. As the car containing Arthur Atkinson and the FBI agent passed through the chain link fence to enter the freeway system, the agent picked up the microphone. Brice Youngmann was advised that Mr. Atkinson was on his way and that they should be at their 20 in approximately 25 minutes.

Samantha always referred to her date as Bernie the Attorney. In fact, his name was Bernard and he was a lawyer who toiled for one of those bankruptcy factories which advertised on television that you could rid yourself of all your problems and achieve nirvana with only $200

down.   It wasn't quite the professional practice which Bernard had imagined, but on the other hand, it sure as hell beat working with his hands.   And, up to a certain point, it was completely legal.

By this time Samantha and Bernie had retired to her apartment where Samantha had deliberately left the thermostat set on 80 degrees to ensure that it would be too warm to keep many clothes on.   They had gotten down to basic underwear and Bernard had proved to Samantha's satisfaction that he was as inept in sexual stimulation as he was in the practice of law.   But, it made no difference whatsoever.   Her script called for getting laid that afternoon and having an otherwise quiet and idyllic day.   Bernard was at hand and Bernard was going to be Mr. Super Stud if she had anything to do with it.

Noting that the clock was moving toward 3:30, Samantha entered the kitchen to pour a couple of glasses of wine,   reappearing dressed with the two wine glasses and nothing else.   Bernard was clearly uncomfortable by the sight of the naked hostess standing before him.   He was almost popping out of his designer boxer shorts.   It didn't take much more coaxing to get him to the bed.   They spent the next hour and 45 minutes wrapped in amorous embrace. Samantha was playing games in her own mind.   "How about that, Harry baby?   We're both getting fucked but I'll bet I'm enjoying it more than you are."

Bernard never did understand why she seemed to have this silly smile at inappropriate times.   He thought perhaps his technique was lacking.   The truth was that his technique was lacking, but it had nothing to do with Samantha's humor.

The beeper on Harry's belt went off as he was continuing his afternoon stroll by Central Park. He ducked into the Ritz Carlton and headed for the pay phone at the back of the lobby. Harry recognized Youngmann's telephone number and dialed it up immediately. "Harry Mills here, what's up?"

"Nothing much, Harry. I've got all of the other players on their way in for the 6 p.m. parlay. I thought maybe if you would like to get here about 10 minutes before that, that you and I might have a private chat and then we'll go into the meeting."

"Yeah, OK, I'll plan to be there at 5:50." At 5:49 p.m. a profusely sweating Harry Mills entered the Federal Building and passed through the metal detectors. He announced himself to the clerk at the desk who politely informed him that an escort would be with him in a moment to take him to Mr. Youngmann. A young woman who appeared to be still in her 20's and dressed in conservative business attire quietly appeared at his side and asked if he had identification. The photo I.D. on her jacket said her name was Janet McCauley. Harry produced his photo I.D.; and, once satisfied, the Ms. McCauley said, "Would you please come with me?" She whisked him through the second security screen and escorted him to an elevator which took him to the floor which housed Youngmann's office and the conference room.

The sign on the door said "Brice Youngmann, SAC." indicating that he was the Special Agent in Charge of this office. The large corner office clearly stated that he was the top dog of the agency in Manhattan. The female agent held the door open for Harry and announced, "Mr. Youngmann, this is Chief Harry Mills of the Midtown Expo Center."

"Thank you. Have a seat Chief Mills. I just need to finish signing these and I'll be right with you."

The female agent withdrew as Harry sat down. Having affixed his signature to a couple of memos, the special agent in charge stuck them in a red file folder and placed them in the out box. He then said to Harry, "Here's what I wanted you to know. In this meeting we have the representatives of every agency which could be involved in this situation. Some of them know more than others. Each one is going to be completely filled in at this meeting and each one is going to move to either grab a piece of the action or run like hell to avoid it. They are going to want to lean on you a bit to find out what you have got up your sleeve to handle this act.

"I can't tell you what to say. That would be unethical. But I can only suggest to you as one brother law enforcement officer to another that at this point the less you say the easier it may be to handle the situation downstream. Making myself understood?"

Harry stood up, "Perfectly. Anything else I need to know?"

"Nope, that's it. Let's go down the hall and face the music." As he spoke, Agent Youngmann placed his hand on Harry's shoulder and guided him toward the door and down the hallway to the waiting conference room.

Youngmann opened the door to the conference room and ushered Harry Mills into a large room containing an oversized conference table, many chairs, blackboards, grease boards, projection equipment and computer terminals. The female agent who had escorted him to Youngmann's office was busy setting out notebooks, pads, pens and water glasses at each one of nine seats which were arranged around the table. In front of each position facing toward the center of the table was a hastily made name placard. Youngmann spoke, "Good afternoon gentlemen. Thank you for being here. I think we better get started."

Each of the attendees found his seat and settled in. At the head of the table, furthest away from the wall which held the projection screen, sat Brice Youngmann. In front of him was a placard that said, Youngmann/FBI. Going around the table clockwise from Youngmann were the seats and signs for Bill Wallace/ATF, Dave Fisher/NYPD, Darryl Jones/NY.State, Harry Mills/Expo Center, Carlton Bentwood/Expo Center, Albert Atkinson/Electronika, Gordon Lewis/NY.State, and Ben Szymanski/Secret Serv.

Harry noticed that all of the men were dressed casually with the exception of the Secret Service man. It seemed to him that guys like Szymanski probably slept in their suits so that they could be ready for any emergency. As soon as the men were seated, Youngmann suggested that each one introduce himself to the others and indicate his position within his agency. Before the others could address the meeting, Youngmann co-opted Harry and Carly and Albert Atkinson by introducing them as civilians and stating their positions with the show and the Expo Center.

Bill Wallace introduced himself as the Resident Chief of the Bureau of Alcohol, Tobacco and Firearms, Darryl Jones was fairly well known to most of them from his anti-terrorism work with the State Police. Gordon Lewis announced that he was a Colonel in the New York State Police and had responsibility for the District which included Manhattan. He had been ordered to attend this meeting by the Director of the State Police and he announced he appeared here as the personal representative of the Director. Dave Fisher announced his position as Deputy Chief of the Tactical Force of the New York City Police Department. He had been ordered to attend this meeting by Margaret Barrows, his Chief. Finally, Ben Szymanski of the Secret Service introduced himself and stated that he had just arrived from Washington within the hour and was on the staff of the White House Protection Unit.

In front of each attendee was a black, half-inch thick ring binder. Youngmann directed each of them to take notice of this binder and told them that this was the situation book containing all of the information which they had to this point. It was completely confidential and copies may be made and distributed only on a need to know basis. In Section 1 of the situation book was a brief statement of what was known at this time. Section 2 included the evidence which was limited to copies of each one of the faxes which had been received from Sam. Section 3 was an assessment of risk which had been made by the Secret Service relating to an appearance by a high executive official at the venue where the show would be held. It had not been updated since 2005. Section 4 was a street map of the area where the Expo Center was located and Section 5 contained a set of detailed drawings of the Expo Center with complete floor plans. Section 6 contained possible suggestions for interagency cooperation and assignments which would be discussed at the meeting.

Youngmann gave a rundown of what they knew and wound up by saying, "In summary, gentlemen, we have a threat to a very important private sector event in our community. At no time has the suspect used the words explosive or bomb or indicated that any explosion would be brought to bear. This inhibits immediate action by the ATF. Local agencies have run thorough background checks and criminal records on every present and past employee of the Expo Center. We have not come up with a single lead to anybody named Sam who remains in this area or who would be considered a suspect. Therefore, we have to assume that whoever Sam is, he has no connection to the Expo Center. We will run the same sort of background on present and former employees of the Electronika exhibit starting tomorrow morning. We do have one videotape which was made at Terminal C of the airport around 3 o'clock this morning. It shows in shadowy form what we believe could possibly be the suspect walking down the hallway, entering the men's room, then leaving the men's room and, we think, entering the area where the coin operated fax machine is located. This is important because the fax machine in the airport is the one from which Exhibit No. 7 was transmitted."

Youngmann paused for a moment and then continued, "We have a problem with the videotape and I'm going to show it to you today while we're here. Then Szymanski will be going back to Washington this evening and will take the tape with him for delivery to the FBI lab tomorrow morning. They will try to enhance this tape to see if we can get a better look at the suspect. The bottom line is that we do not know who the suspect is. We don't know what he wants, we don't know what cause he represents, we don't know what kind of device he intends to use, and we don't know which day of this show he plans to attack. On the other hand, we do know that we have 100,000 visitors who will be attending this show, we have ill-trained and inadequately equipped security personnel at the Expo Center, and we have the Vice President of the United States planning to give the keynote speech on the opening day of this exhibition."

The men seated around the table were each busily scribbling notes on the yellow pads which lay in front of them. Brice Youngmann spoke again, "I'd like to go around the table and ask each of you to give us the benefit of your questions or thoughts from the perspective of your own agency or company. Why don't you start, Ben?"

Ben Szymanski cleared his throat, took off his glasses and carefully laid them on the table in front of him. "Well as you guys know, our job in this particular unit is confined to protecting the life and well being of the Chief Executive, the Vice President and their immediate families. We are not directly concerned with catching loonies and particularly in this case we have a problem because there have been no threats made against the Vice President directly. I checked through these exhibits and nowhere does this guy mention that he is going to try to take out the Vice President. So here's my problem. I don't have any jurisdiction to go hunting for this guy."

Szymanski continued, "Now that I've laid all

that out for the record, we will of course do everything we can to help the situation. Personally I'd be just as happy if Rosebud decided to stay home and forget the whole damn thing. He could always catch a cold or get a hangnail or be assigned to go up to the UN and make nice to some third world potentate."

Carlton Bentwood, III sat calmly with his fingertips placed against each other and pressing in and out like a spider doing pushups on a mirror. He said not a word to Harry Mills who sat at his right.

Dave Fisher from the Police Department was the next to address the group saying, "Well guys, I don't really know much about this and I just got a call from Chief Barrows about an hour and a half ago. It looks like we're being called in at the last minute and I don't think that we had any information whatsoever from the Secret Service about the Vice President's appearance here in town or from any of the rest of you guys about the threat against this show and this facility. That being the case, I'm not sure what we can do this late in the game but, of course, the facilities of the Police Department are available and we will give this top priority."

What went through the minds of most of the people sitting at the table is that top priority by the Police Department was roughly equivalent to the matter being given top priority by the Sarajevo Police Department. Any one of the federal agencies had ten times as much muscle and backup as the NYPD. It was well known to each one of the people in the room, but in order to observe the proprieties of the situation and keep from ruffling political feathers, they had to be brought into the picture. They

could, at least, provide crowd control in the registration
lines and in the traffic lanes outside the building.

Albert Atkinson raised his hand and was
acknowledged by Brice Youngmann. He cleared his throat
and asked if he might address this group. "I am Albert
Atkinson as you have been told. I am the President of
Electronika Internationale. What I've heard in this room
today is absolutely shocking. I can tell you that we have
gone to very great pains to provide for the security of our
exhibitors and our attendees at our shows. We have never
had an incident where there has been any major criminal
activity or disruption of an event which we have produced.
I can also tell you that the appearance of the Vice President
at our exhibition this coming week was arranged by request
of very influential members of Congress and I believe that
it would be in very poor taste for the Vice President not to
be able to appear. Certainly nobody wants anyone to put
himself in jeopardy, but we can't have the rest of the world
thinking that we are afraid of our own shadow, can we?"

Szymanski knew what Atkinson was talking
about. Atkinson's company was owned by a wealthy
offshore multi-national conglomerate. They called in some
IOU's from a few senators who they had helped to put into
business who in turn prevailed upon the Vice President to
show up at this show. The prestige which the appearance
of the Vice President would lend to this show was
immeasurable. It probably was second only to an
appearance by somebody like Bill Gates or Madonna and
that prestige translated into several more million bucks in
Atkinson's pocket. He really couldn't have cared less about
the Vice President and probably didn't even know where he
came from.

Atkinson looked directly at Bentwood and Mills as he said, "Of course, security is ultimately the responsibility of the management of the Expo Center. We look to them to provide the necessary levels of security, and to cooperate with your various agencies, and we will hold them ultimately responsible for this function. There is very little that we can add to this function and to the extent that we have any input in the security of the show, we shall be glad to cooperate in any manner possible."

It was a nice job of not only passing the buck to the Expo Center, but handing Carlton Bentwood one hot potato that he was ill-equipped to handle. If anything went drastically wrong at the Electronika Internationale Exhibition, he might kiss not only the exhibition goodbye, but very possibly his own job. The message certainly wasn't lost on Harry Mills either.

Youngmann addressed his next question to Ben Szymanski, "Ben, it looks as though my agency will probably have to take the lead on this until the Vice President's visit is announced or confirmed, would you agree with that?"

"Yes and no, Brice. Here's the situation from our perspective. We have a provisional notification that the Vice President will be here. His office makes the announcements, as you know. They haven't done so yet. We don't have a confirmed threat against his person so we cannot step in and recommend to him any change in his plans. On the other hand, I do need to make certain that our agency covers its ass by forwarding the information to the Office of the Vice President that there has been a threat against the show. As you can imagine, we have to start moving right now to make certain that should he delay the announcement and make a last minute decision, that we are not disabled. Therefore, we are going to treat this as a normal visit by the Vice President to any venue. At the time that the announcement is made, we will then probably escalate the status of the visit and increase our control activities." Szymanski continued, "Therefore, I am making an authorized request to each of you at this table to keep my office informed of all matters relating to this threat against the show. In turn, we will feed back anything that we can supply through Brice's office. So to that extent, while not abandoning our charter to protect the Vice President, I do agree that it would be best if Brice leads the show at this time."

"Let me help you focus on the venue," said Youngmann. He lowered the lights in the room and turned on the projector. On the far wall a schematic diagram of the Expo Center was displayed with the adjacent streets and parking areas clearly visible. "The area which is shown in red is the area actually used by the Electronika show. The visitors enter on this side of the building and pass through registration desks where they then are directed into the main exhibit halls. As you can see, there are eight main public accesses to the exhibit halls and eight banks of elevators, escalators and stairs. As a result, we have a difficult problem in putting screening devices at each area although we intend to do so." Atkinson was starting to squirm in his chair at the thought of airport-type security at his show.

"If you will look at the areas that are marked in yellow, those are the areas through which the Vice President would have to pass coming in through the lower

111

level entrance and being conveyed by the service area ways to the meeting hall where he would give a speech and presumably would exit in the same fashion. The areas outside the building, which I marked in blue, are those areas which would fall under local police jurisdiction, being the local Police Department, and the State Police. We will work with you to help coordinate our investigation to make certain that this threat is not carried through."

Lewis wasn't paying a whole lot of attention. His agency was being relegated to providing traffic cop duty which is basically all they ever did unless they were on special detail such as protecting the governor or working inside the hall on a per diem basis. But, it was Dave Fisher who put Harry in the hot seat. "Chief Mills, what are your plans to control the perimeter and the interior of the building?" Harry started to squirm in his chair and cleared his voice hesitantly as if to speak, when Brice Youngmann replied, "Chief Mills is in a position where he has indicated that he would like to have our input to help design an overall plan. I don't believe we have agreed yet on the final plan, have we Chief?"

"No, in fact, I expected that we would meet perhaps tomorrow to finish that, Mr. Youngmann." Harry was off the grill for this time but clearly he had to do something. The question was quickly becoming, what could he do that would be effective? He knew the answer. Damn little.

Brice clicked the projector remote control and changed the image to a closeup of the loading docks of the Expo Center. "Here's where the fun begins. This is a shot of the loading dock area of the center. Starting

112

tomorrow, these 20 loading bays will start receiving somewhere in the neighborhood of 400 trailer loads of goods for the exhibit. Each one of those semis will be filled with electronic equipment. We don't have enough officers here who have background in weapons detection and explosive detection to go through every one of these pieces of equipment without delaying the opening of the show. We are bringing in a team from Washington and we're also bringing in selected agents from other cities who will be here starting tomorrow.

"One problem we know is that the truckers are going to be mad as hell because of delays in off-loading. They're going to be pissed off at the demurrage and that means other truckers are going to be backed up all over the local streets waiting to get to the loading docks.

"What some of you may not know is that when a show like this is organized, these truckers are given appointment times when they should be available to pull into the dock. They're allowed to stay there for an appropriate amount of time to off-load. Now if we delay each one of them by several hours, we're going to have one hell of a problem."

At that point Dave Fisher interjected, "Well, we're going to have a hell of a problem with traffic control with all of those tractor trailers hanging around in what is essentially a no stopping, no parking area. I'm also kind of curious how we are going to keep this away from the press because the bastards are all over the place."

Youngmann continued, "We'll address the question of the press in a few minutes. However, I agree there is going to be one hell of a traffic problem created by all these trailer trucks and we have no practical way to contact these rigs to get them to lay-by at some remote area such as the airport. If we could, we would set up a temporary screening area away from the hall but that is out of the question. One further consideration is that the people who own these loads are not accused of doing anything nor are they suspected of doing anything illegal. They're going to start screaming bloody murder because they have crews coming in to set up their exhibits. I also assume that in the case of some of the more sophisticated electronic equipment, that they don't want anybody to even touch the stuff and to be quite honest we wouldn't know what the hell it is to begin with."

Youngmann clicked the remote control again and this time an image zoomed in showing all of the accesses into the exhibition halls. "To continue this Nightmare on 13th Street scenario, folks, take a look at this. I want you to notice the number of stairwells, escalators, loading doors and service accesses into these halls. What we're looking at is more than 60 of them. I haven't checked with any of the state fire marshals but you can bet your bippy we can't close down very many of these entrances. In fact, I don't want to close any of them because if something does blow up in this hall, I want the people to be able to get out just as quickly as they can through every one of these egresses."

Youngmann turned to Harry Mills, "Chief Mills, do your people wear photo I.D.'s?"

"No Sir, they don't."

"Well, do you have the equipment to provide them?"

Harry admitted that they had no such equipment and that they had never bothered to use photo ID's for any of their help. At this point Youngmann offered to make the equipment available on loan from his agency. Ben Szymanski offered that should the Vice President be coming to the event, all of the workers who would be coming into contact or close proximity to the Vice President would require Secret Service clearance and photo I.D.'s to be worn on lanyards.

Youngmann then turned to Dave Fisher and asked, "Chief Fisher, do you have authority to close off these four streets which I've marked in green on the chart for the next few days so that we can do some outside inspection of these tractor trailers before they get to the loading dock?"

Fisher replied, "We have limited emergency powers. I can close them off if you ask me to and I will just pass the buck to you. Here again, it will take about three minutes for the press to hop all over it."

"Ok guys, let's talk about the press," said Youngmann. "My office has been contacted by a fella by the name of Bates from The New York Ledger. He advises me that he has contacted other law enforcement agencies to determine whether or not there is any truth to a so-called rumor about an attack on the Electronika show. At this point if your agency has been contacted by Bates that you know of, would you please indicate that by raising your hand." Five hands went up indicating that each one of the agencies involved had been similarly contacted by the diligent Mr. Bates.

Brice put his idea forward. "I have a suggestion I'd like to ask you to consider. We need to have a coordinated answer made to the press. At this point, the press feels that we are dealing with a bomb threat. For that reason, I think that we should have the PIO at ATF handle all requests for information from the press and Bill can refer them to his information officer who can hand out whatever the party line is going to be on a daily basis. Is there anybody here that has a problem with that?"

Seeing that there was no objection forthcoming from anyone at the table, it was agreed and the stage was set for the Public Information Office at the Bureau of Alcohol, Tobacco and Firearms to become the official spokesagency for the coordinated attack. By doing so, the other agencies hoped that they would either escape the heat should their counterattack fail, or be left alone to continue their efforts without bringing to the attention of the public that their agency had been called in.

It was Youngmann who wound up the meeting. "Take a look at the last section in your books and the first page has on it a series of direct monitored telephone numbers for each one of us and our designated deputies within our agencies. Those telephone lines will be open and monitored at all times. We also have fax numbers here and there is a computer access which is for restricted use that will go to a user group or a home page or whatever you want to call it on the government net that any of our agencies can tap in on. We can leave messages for each other there. I've got my beeper on at all times and my office knows how to contact me. Presumably the same is true of each of you. As of 1200 hours today, we have canceled all leaves in our agency. We are on a full alert status and I'm asking you guys to stick around, to stand with us, and let's do whatever we can to make sure that this is stopped before it goes any further. Does anybody have anything else he wants to add?"

Darryl Jones spoke up. "Well, let's summarize it Brice. Right now we don't know who this kook is but we're trying to ID the suspect. We don't know the device to be used and that's agreed upon and we got one bitch of a job protecting this venue without closing down the show. Personally my life would be a lot easier if this show would just pick up and go somewhere else, but I guess we can't do that. You did mention that you were going to roll the videotape for us and I'm curious to see it."

"Thank you," said Youngmann. He turned off the slide projector and activated the videotape projector. A murky black and white image came on the screen. "You can see this figure walking down the hall in Concourse C and you can note the time in the top right corner is 2:48 a.m. There you see the figure turning to go into what apparently is the men's room and I'm going to fast forward at this point because there is a couple minutes of dead tape. Now you see what we believe is the same figure coming out. Now the figure is walking toward the camera. Let me stop this here and freeze frame. There's our problem.

What you see is nothing but a shadow outline figure. I can't make out anything on the face here. Now take a look at this." Youngmann put the tape back on play and they saw the figure proceed toward the camera another 15 or 20 paces and turn to its left where it disappeared off the screen.

"Now let me fast forward some more because the figure is in what we believe is this alcove where the fax machine is located for four and one-half minutes. The subject then emerges again and continues on to the stairs that go down." Youngmann ran the tape forward until he got to the appropriate place and played the part of the tape showing the shadowy figure leaving the hallway.

"I've got several copies of this tape and I'll make it available to anyone who wants it. But, as I said, this original is going north with Ben in about hour. By tomorrow morning we'll know whether or not the whiz kids in the lab have been able to enhance the tape.

"Oh yeah," said Youngmann, "Mr. Bentwood, I think it would be a great help if you would provide a temporary operations center for us at your facility and I plan to move four of my people in there this afternoon. We will need direct telephone lines and fax lines which we will have installed this afternoon. We will provide our own security. I figure we are going to need for a combined operation like this somewhere in the neighborhood of 1,000 square feet. Can you handle that on such short notice?"

"Yes Sir, I can. I don't know if it's 1,000 square feet but we'll give you whatever accommodations you need including shutting down one of the small breakout areas for your use. Harry, will you take care of that please?" It was a rhetorical question which did not require Harry's response other than to nod his head as he made some notes on his pad. The meeting was soon over and each of the participants went their separate ways with the exception of Carlton Bentwood who asked Harry Mills to join him at a nearby restaurant for a cup of coffee.

10

While the various state and federal agents were joined in their meeting, Samantha was joined in hers with her friend Bernie. She had an innate sense of time and without looking at the clock, knew that it was somewhere between 5:15 and 5:30. Time to get Bernie off, up, dressed and out.

She feigned a phone call to an imaginary aunt and while the telephone was playing the weather report in her ear, she was confirming that indeed she would leave by 6 p.m. and be at auntie's by 6:30 or 6:40 without fail. At 5:55 p.m., Bernie and Samantha left the apartment. They each drove off in different directions. Samantha made sure she wasn't being followed and then headed directly to the Expo Center to see what was happening there.

Driving past the Expo Center, she noticed that there were three or four cars she hadn't seen before. Each one of these cars was a four-door sedan, dark-colored with plain black-wall tires, the usual trademark of a police vehicle. She didn't notice any large antennae on the rear end of the cars and without the use of a pair of binoculars, couldn't tell whether they had little rat tails on the rear decks. In any event, she didn't want to be observed using binoculars in this area nor stopping to check out these cars more closely. Satisfied that there was an increased level of some police activity at the Expo Center, Samantha cruised off toward Harry Mills' home to check on the level of activity there. She found that nothing unusual was going on and being a little disappointed, decided that he must have been active back at the Expo Center.

Dinner that evening consisted of a three piece chicken dinner with biscuits and honey from a local fast food joint. Samantha thought to herself, "If you're going crazy waiting, Harry Baby, think what it's doing to me." The ennui of sitting out these hours until the next phase of her plan went into motion was taking its toll on her otherwise placid personality. "Its time to get the plot rolling a bit." thought Samantha.

In the trunk of the car was the new fax machine which she had purchased from a chain discount office supply store. She had paid cash for the unit and carefully preserved the packing materials and owner's manual so she could return it in the 30-day grace period and get a cash refund without leaving any trail that would have her name connected to it. In any event, even if somebody should link her to the faxes, the fax machine would have been rotated back into stock and sold to any one of thousands of customers who frequent that store on a weekly basis.

This time Samantha sought out a different university in the suburbs where she found the same accommodating bank of computers and printers that she had enjoyed previously. She tapped out messages for the managing editor of the newspaper and for Carlton Bentwood. Samantha packed up her messages and got back in the car for a 30-minute drive to another suburban area where she parked in the visitors parking lot of a local hospital.

Nobody took notice of the young woman with the heavy briefcase who walked purposefully toward the maternity waiting room. All sorts of strange people sat out the interminable minutes and hours in maternity waiting rooms while they tried to maintain their lives as normally as possible. So nobody paid any attention to the young woman with the fax machine in her briefcase. She plugged into a nearby outlet and then connected to the courtesy phone on the counter by the couch. Samantha zapped off the fax to the newspaper and then dialed up the number for the fax machine in Carlton Bentwood's office. On the front of the fax machine was a liquid crystal display window that showed the status of the fax and when the number was connected, the station identification of the number to which the fax was being sent.

When transmitting to Bentwood's machine, she expected to see MDTN EXPO CTR appear in the screen. Instead, what she saw was a message that had been placed there by Darryl Jones. The screen showed "**SAM 212-924-8867**." What was this? Samantha studied it carefully. It clearly had been placed there for her benefit and it looked like a local telephone number. Samantha scribbled the number on a scrap of paper and stuck it in the pocket of her blouse. When her transmissions were done, she casually, but without delay, unhooked the machine from the telephone and the electricity and tried to look as if she were really interested in the article she was reading in Time magazine. In another few minutes she casually got up and with her briefcase clutched in her right hand, walked slowly out of the maternity waiting room and down the hall to retrieve her car. She would not visit this hospital again. Every animal instinct in her body was tensed with the smell of entrapment. Whoever programmed the fax machine in

Bentwood's office wanted her to call that phone number. She had to do it, she knew.

Samantha drove to a nearby hotel where she knew there was a bank of telephones near a stairway that led to a lower level. She could exit through the pool without having to come through the lobby again. She took a small pad of paper and a pen with her into the hotel. When Samantha heard the "Thank you for choosing AT&T" she dialed up the number and waited for it to ring. What she heard was Darryl's voice in a pre-recorded message.

"Sam, do not hang up, this is an unattended message. Please listen carefully and this call is not being traced. This is Darryl Jones of the State Police. I know that you are unhappy with the people who promote the Electronika Internationale Show and I don't blame you for wanting to point out their greed and excesses. I'm certain you have important things that you want to say and I want to help you say them. I'd like for us to establish some kind of communication so that we can talk to each other. I really do understand your needs and I want to know more about you. I can promise you that you will not be hurt, I will not try to take you into custody and I will not put tracers on any calls that you make to me. Please write down the following telephone number. It is an unlisted number which I have had installed that will go directly to me at any time that you want to call. If I'm not available, it will automatically switch over to a cellular phone which I will have with me at all times."

Samantha wrote down the number as requested. The recording continued by saying, "As evidence of my sincerity and that this message is intended only for you, Sam, the number which you saw displayed on your fax machine is being changed every day and this message is being changed every day until you acknowledge that you have received the message. You can acknowledge now by pressing <u>one</u> on your telephone. This concludes the outgoing messages." Samantha pressed in on the <u>one</u> key. then quickly disconnected and exited the hotel through the pool area.

If she could have imitated the guys in the Toyota commercials who jump for joy about six feet off the ground, she would gladly have done so. Samantha was elated. The game was on and now the cops were willing to play the game with her. She had to think how she would want to proceed at this point. Obviously, there was another phone number that she had to call. She didn't believe for an instant that the police officer understood her, because she didn't understand herself. She knew damn well that he was lying when he said he wouldn't try to take her into custody and she knew that he was lying when he said that he wouldn't try to trace the call. By now, there were at least two or three unmarked police cars on their way to this hotel and they would be coming in the front door while she was leaving by the pool exit. She must remember to obey the speed limits.

Actually, Darryl hadn't bothered to put automatic traces to the recording machine. That was going to be of no value. He knew that Sam was too slick to fall for the usual routine of staying on the line and being chatted up by a policeman while 10 other cops descended upon him to effect the arrest. This was clearly somebody who had to be handled in a negotiating situation.

Samantha was drawn to make the call in the same manner that a chocoholic is drawn to dessert. She wanted it. She needed to do it. She couldn't avoid doing it. She also knew that the call was fraught with danger. In this circumstance, the best location for her was that labyrinth of hotels, shops and exhibit spaces that are clustered together in Soho. There were pay phones, and in the event that the area were flooded with police, she could simply leave by one of the side doors or the older buildings and depart unobtrusively.

Samantha knew that her best defense was to keep whatever telephone contact was made to less than two minutes. If they had caller ID, which she was sure they were using, it would take police at least two minutes to respond to a call. This was not something that they were going to dispatch the local beat cop to handle. Samantha found the phones which she wanted near a restaurant and dialed up the number.

It was another recorded message and this was just the sort of thing which she was enjoying. It was Darryl Jones again. The message was, "Sam, I am very glad you have called. This machine has the ability to record some responses from you and I would appreciate it if you would help me to help you. First, let me repeat again to you my pledge that I am not tracing the source of this call, I do not want to arrest you, I do want to help you and I do want to provide a forum to you to publicize your position and/or your grievances. But I need a little input from you. Please tell me are you willing to meet with me face to face? Please give me your response after the beep and press the pound sign when you are done speaking."

Samantha had no intention of providing a voice exemplar to the police. She pressed the pound sign which activated the next part of the outgoing message. "I would like to know if you can give me a telephone number even if it is a phone booth where I can call you and give me a time when I can call you. I promise you that I will make the call and maybe we can set up an appointment for a personal meeting. Please give me your answer after the beep and press the pound sign when you are done speaking." Again, Samantha pressed the pound sign, "Nice try," thought Samantha.

The message picked up again, "Sam, if it is money you want, please know that I am authorized to meet your demands no matter what they are. Just tell me how much it is, in what form you need it and when you want it and how you want it and it will be done. You can go ahead and speak at the beep and just press the pound sign when you are done." Again, Samantha pressed the pound sign. She had to admit to herself that this opened up a whole new vista of negotiation which she had never thought of before. Was her plan worth a couple of hundred thousand dollars to them? If so, that might make her middle age quite a bit more comfortable. On the other hand, she would be denied the joy of seeing this show totally disrupted.

The tape continued, "Sam, please write down this fax number that I am about to give you. The number will be repeated twice for you and if you wish to have this entire message repeated, press 7 at the conclusion of the recording. The fax number is one which you can use to communicate with me privately at any time and just like this phone call, it will not be traced. There are no tricks here. The number is 212-924-4113. Sam, I thank you for listening to this. I want to repeat again to you that I am your friend and I want to help you. If you wish to have this outgoing message repeated from the beginning, please press 7 at any time. If you would like to leave your message for me on any subject, you may press 4 and then speak as long as you wish up to 15 minutes. Please press the pound sign when you are done speaking and if you wish to terminate this call at this time, press 3 or simply hang up." Samantha pressed 3 and then hung up. She strolled casually the six blocks to her car.

In the Grill Room of the hotel, Carlton Bentwood, III had a quiet talk with Harry. "Harry, this thing is getting to be bigger than the both of us. Atkinson caught me before the meeting and I agreed that you would fly up to Chicago this evening with his pilot and meet a Mr. Casey, who is his chief of security. Casey will fly back here with you; and the reason why I want you on the plane is I don't want to waste any time. I want you to brief Casey completely on what you've heard today, take your situation book with you and, in fact, try to make a copy of it for him before you meet the guy. We need for you and him to cooperate fully and as far as these cops are concerned, we want to push as much of this as possible on them, but we have to make it look as though we are breaking our backs to do everything humanly possible. You understand, Harry, that if the shit hits the fan, it has to be their fault, not ours."

For once, his boss seemed to be thinking clearly. "He certainly knows how to cover his own ass." thought Harry.

"Yes Sir, I just want to call my wife and tell her that I'm going to be late tonight and not to worry. Where do I meet this plane?"

"The pilot's name is Tom Nichols and you meet him at the Teterboro FBO office. He'll be expecting you at 9:30 this evening. That will put you into Chicago by about 10:30 their time and you should be back here by 1 or 2 a.m.."

By 10 o'clock Sunday evening, the control center had been set up at the Expo building. Brice Youngmann had a large map of the area on the wall with numbered colored markers positioned on the map. Each map indicated a known location where telecommunications had been initiated to either the newspaper or Harry from Sam. It was infuriating for him to regard this map because there seemed to be absolutely no pattern whatsoever to the locations. Furthermore, Youngmann had the gnawing suspicion that Sam might actually be more than one person. If it were two or more people acting in unison, it was going to be much more difficult to crack this case. The telephone lines and the fax lines which had been provided to Sam were now all terminating at the control center for what would become known as Operation Boomtown.

Brice had reprogrammed the fax machine and the auto responder a few minutes before another call came from Sam. After Sam had connected to the machine, what she heard was, "You have reached a private voice and fax facility which has been organized for the restricted use of one individual. In order to gain access you are requested to spell out the first three letters of your first name. If access is denied, this call will terminate." Samantha pressed the buttons for 7, 2, and 5 to spell out Sam and was connected to the next voice mailbox in the chain which told her that from now on a private numeric code would be required to access any communications to ensure complete privacy. She was asked to enter a five-digit numeric code which in the future would grant her private access and control over these facilities. Sam completed the entries according to the request.

The voice message gave out the recorded spiel. "If you wish to transmit a fax, press 5, if you wish to leave a voice message, press 6 and speak until completed, then press the pound sign or hang up. If you wish to speak to an attendant at this time, press 1 and stand by, your call will be routed to Special Agent Brice Youngmann for response." Samantha had the acoustic coupler set up and transmitted her latest fax to Youngmann. As the fax was being printed out in Youngmann's control center, he took a look at it and muttered a curse under his breath. "This bastard is one piece of work." The fax from Sam said simply, "We will have no verbal communication. I would be happy to answer questions, but only if you phrase them

129

in such a way that I can respond by pressing one or two keys on a touch tone telephone. No communication connection will last more than two minutes. Finally, and as a matter of idle curiosity, just how much is it worth to the Electronika people for me to get lost?" The fax ended with a typed signature that simply said, "Sam."

Youngmann wrote down the telephone number from which the call had originated and punched it into the computer which stood near the telecom equipment. The number belonged to a coin telephone at a convenience store in Harlem.. This was an area of lower income homes which were predominantly African American. Was he looking for a black person? He had no idea. Of course, looking for a black person in Harlem would simply limit the suspects to a few hundred thousand. This wasn't a leap of logic which he was prepared to undertake. For one thing, the events of recent cases in other states had led him to be sensitive to hastily nominating any minority as a miscreant without very hard evidence. Furthermore, there was very little historical evidence of black people taking part in terrorist activities aimed at the general public. It was far more likely that he was dealing with an individual sociopath or an organized group such as a *jihad*.

Captain Nichols turned on the Fasten Your Seat Belt lights and let loose the brakes on the Gulfstream under his command. It bounced down the runway and was soon free of the earth and headed in an easterly direction making for New Jersey. Although Red Casey had flown many times on the corporate jet, this was the first experience that Harry had ever had of living among the real jet set. Once they were airborne, the seat belt sign was taken off and Captain Nichols advised his two passengers through the PA system that the bar was open and would they please help themselves to whatever they cared to have. Their flying time to Jersey would be one hour and 50 minutes. It had been a tough day for Harry Mills. He poured himself an overly generous glass of Jack Daniels and splashed in a few drops of water so that he might appear to be a bit more moderate in his habits. Casey twisted off the cap of a Budweiser and the two men settled down in the large captain's chairs across from each other with a fold down working table between them.

After feeling out each other as to their professional backgrounds and their common experiences and who they might know and where, Harry pushed toward Casey a file folder which contained a series of copies which he had made at a local quick print. This was the situation book for Operation Boomtown. As Harry started to explain the situation and fill Red in on everything which he knew, he was met by unbelieving stares, the occasional "Jesus," and every so often a low whistling sound which Casey made by expelling air through his wide-set lower teeth.

By the time the Lektra-I had set down, the two security men had thoroughly briefed each other on what they felt they could each contribute to control this maddening situation.

By that time, Samantha had tucked herself in for the night. She had work to do the next morning and was expected in the office at 8 a.m. In fact, Samantha had to get quite a bit done on Monday, Tuesday and Wednesday because she had scheduled a personal day off on Thursday. She had a 9 a.m. appointment with her dentist for a cleaning and had scheduled a 10:30 appointment at her OB/GYN for her annual checkup. Once having satisfied the requirements of going to these appointments in order to substantiate the need for a personal day off, she would have the rest of the day free and thought that she might stop in at the Electronika Internationale Expo. She had mentioned this to one of her co-workers who opined that she was crazy to take personal time to go research stuff that could be used for the company; when, if she asked her boss, they might simply give her a day off to go to the show.

Samantha was early for work and picked up a copy of The Ledger in the lobby of the office building when she arrived at a little past seven. She often showed up early and took her breakfast in the little coffee shop off the lobby.

Her reaction to this morning's newspaper was highly controlled inasmuch as she was in a place where she might be observed by others. But along with her coffee, bagel and orange juice, she took a look at the front page of the newspaper and was amazed by what she saw. There were two front page articles with equal space running head to head. The first announced, "Electronika opens

132

Thursday. 100,000 Expected." The article went on to detail how this very important trade show would bring millions of dollars and tens of thousands of visitors to her city.

The article which was to the right of it, and which is the more important position on the page, was headlined, "Veep to Address Electronika Despite Bomb Threat." The article then went on to relate everything which had happened so far which Samantha had orchestrated. But the article also contained five small photographs one column wide by about two inches high each of the five state and federal agency chiefs who had met on Saturday. The article even indicated that an emergency control center had been organized at the Expo Center and was being operated under the code name of Operation Boomtown.

Well, she had wanted to match wits with the best and the brightest and she certainly was getting more than she asked for. It seemed that everybody other than the forest rangers had been called in to marshal their resources against one five foot three woman. The poor dears didn't realize that they were undermanned.

The day passed uneventfully at work for Samantha. She had the usual banter with her fellow workers and put out a bit more than the usual amount of work expected of her. She had taken a lunch hour in the company of two colleagues and they had discussed their weekends. Samantha titillated them by recounting her Sunday afternoon tryst with Bernie the Attorney. Nothing untoward occurred during the workday although every fiber of her body itched with anxiety and desire to get back into the game. She wanted desperately to fire off another fax to Brice Youngmann. She wanted to tweak the newspaper editor and more than anything else, she wanted to pull Harry Mills' chain again. Four-thirty finally came and she was free of her daily labors. She casually packed up and left the building to make the evening trip back to her apartment.

While Samantha had been working at her office, the minions of the law had been hard at work down at the Expo Center. At 0700 the first of the 18-wheelers had started to back down onto the loading docks to disgorge it's cargo of exhibition booths and ultra-sophisticated electronic gear. At first, none of the drivers noticed the heightened level of security. They didn't think it unusual that as each rig came in a record was made of the markings, license plates, and the identification of each driver was requested. What they didn't know is that when the security guard took the commercial driver's license into his guard house, that he passed it under a scanner which immediately fed the image and all the data to an FBI monitor at Operation Boomtown. Four of the workers in coveralls who were seen on the loading docks were FBI agents. Nor did the drivers seem concerned that as the goods were off loaded, one of the attendants on the loading dock insisted that every crate and every item be identified with a serially numbered tag which was affixed to the container or the item. A record was being made of everything that was off-loaded so that it could be identified as to the carrier that brought it to the loading dock. Slowly, the materials were passed through into the main exhibit hall. For some reason, only two of the large access doors seemed to be open and working, and each one of these doors was manned by at least three or four employees who were doing nothing but standing around watching the goods coming in. Still, that could just be normal feather-bedding by a quasi-governmental agency.

Once inside the hall, it was obvious that this was anything but a normal situation. In fact, there were teams of agents with dogs roaming the hall and all exits from the hall were barred except one which had a magnamometer set up to scan everything going through to the hallway. All of the lavatories had been locked down except for one men's room which had an attendant in it. What the workers couldn't see is that during the night a battery of 32 additional closed circuit television cameras had been installed in this hall which scanned every inch of the hall and each one was connected to a recording machine which made a permanent record. Of the 60 coin phones located in and about the hall, every one of them had a line tap on it. Further, microphones had been installed in all of the lavatories which were along the perimeter of the exhibit hall. The government did not feel that it could install closed circuit videos in these facilities but they sure as hell were going to listen in.

Outside the exhibit hall, the main access areas to the center were locked down except for one door which had a magnamometer surrounding it and was manned by two police officers. Nobody from the general public would be allowed in. Anyone who appeared from one of the exhibiting companies had to produce positive identification, was photographed and issued a photo ID badge. They were also issued a color coded wristband like those used in hospitals which identified them as being allowed into a specified area on that particular date. The orders were not to admit anyone from the media. Seven or eight reporters and photographers were hanging around the outside door to the facility and getting angrier by the moment. Four television film trucks were parked at the curb and cameras were set up trained on the doors. Clearly, this was going to be the lead story in every news broadcast until some answers were forthcoming and, unfortunately, there were no answers at this time.

The airport security police had cooperated fully with the federal agents when they requested that they cordon off that area of Terminal C which had been videotaped Saturday night. The agents quickly had somebody reenact what they had seen. One of the agents put on an overcoat and walked into view of the television camera and continued on, walking straight ahead and then turning right into the men's room. He waited in the men's room the exact amount of time that the person had been seen waiting on the previous tape and then emerged and walked back for the same length of stride and turned to his left. He took eight steps and wound up standing against a blank wall. Assuming that something was wrong with the agent and that he had perhaps walked too quickly or taken too long a stride, he was requested to do another take for the tape. This time he altered the length of his stride and slowed down his pace. He wound up again at a blank wall. What the hell was going on? The Feds obtained the tape from the security office of the airport and gave them their thanks for their splendid cooperation. That tape was at Operation Boomtown by 11 a.m.

At this time, Darryl Jones was also in the operations center and he placed a call to the lab in Washington to find out how they were doing with enhancing the images. The answer that came back didn't fill him with joy. There was no way that they could enhance the image. The cameras used by the airport were low quality, inexpensive cameras which were very grainy and did not have a sufficiently fast enough lens to allow them to enhance the image. When the lab tech in Washington asked Darryl what he thought ought to be done with the tape, Darryl suppressed his normal inclination which was to tell him to insert it where the sun doesn't shine. He told them to just hang on to it since he had additional copies on hand.

Darryl gave one of the copies of the original tape, together with the original of this newly made exemplar, to Janet McCauley who was working in the room. "Do you think we could get these up on two different tape players and put them onto the same size adjoining screens so we could look at them for comparative purposes?

She replied, "Will do."

A few minutes later. the several agents in the room sat scratching their heads as they observed the two monitors. On the left was the tape which they presumed was the suspect observed on the airport video cams from two days earlier. On the right were the two tapes which had been made this morning at the airport. On a table in front of them was a copy of a blueprint of Terminal C which they had procured from airport operations.

It was Agent Janet McCauley who asked, "Were these two tapes generated from the same fixed position camera?" Upon hearing that they were, she said, "I got to tell you, I don't think you're looking for a guy." She took the two remote control units for the two tape players in her hands and froze each one of them at the point where the suspect and the agent emerged from the men's room. "Look at the relative sizes of those images. The one on the right seems to be a lot taller. Who's the agent?" Brice answered that it was one of the FBI guys, named Ken. "How tall is he?" asked Janet. "I'd say he's about 5' 10" said Brice. "Well," said Janet. "If he's 5' 10", then our suspect must be a midget. My guess is our subject is a woman. Now you say he kept walking into the wall when Ken made these tapes?"

"Correct."

"How do you know that the subject in the first tape went into the men's room? Take a look at this floor plan. If he went into the ladies room, the door is about 35 feet away from the entrance to the mens room. Both of the lavatories back up to each other but the entrances are at the furthest end of each, correct?"

"Yeah, go ahead," said Brice.

"Then if our suspect went into the ladies room and came out and walked forward the same number

138

of paces, look where 35 feet further down the hall would put our suspect." The men gathered around and looked at the floor plan. She was absolutely right. It would have put the suspect right in front of the telephone alcove. It was almost in unison that they muttered, "Son of a bitch."

Youngmann turned to Janet, "Janet, I want you to take my car and get yourself out to the airport immediately. I want you to replicate this tape again with the same deal. I want you to go into the ladies room, hang in there for the same length of time, come out walk down and turn into the telephone alcove and I want you back here as fast as possible. I'll call down to the airport and make the arrangements for you. Get going."

Youngmann wasn't inclined to impede the career of a brother agent just because the brother might be a sister. But, back when J. Edgar ran the shop things were a whole lot different. Blacks, Latinos, Asians and women would have been glad to find a glass ceiling. Hoover had made it damn near impossible for them to gain advancement of any type. Youngmann had to admit that Janet was something else. She came from a wealthy Republican family in Old Lyme, Connecticut. She had majored in Romance Languages at Bryn Mawr and after being graduated she signed on with the Peace Corps. Eschewing a lush post in rural France, Janet volunteered for work in southeast Asia.

When she came home, she had a different world view. Janet got admitted to Harvard Law School where she was graduated *cum laude* and won a post on their prestigious Law Review. She was brilliant, and everyone who knew her family thought she would go right

139

from Harvard Square to Wall Street to start making megabucks on mega-deals. The few friends who really knew Janet were not surprised when she applied for a job with the FBI. She possessed a rare combination of intellect, drive, and humanity that her fellow agents quickly came to respect and admire. If there were to be a Mother Teresa of the FBI; it would surely be Mother Janet one day.

By the time Janet left the room, Brice was on the telephone to airport security. The terminal hallway would be cordoned off once again and another test tape would be made.

11

      There was a palpable nervousness among Harry Mills' crew on Monday. They could read English and they had seen the stories in the newspaper. Those who didn't read had seen it on television. Something dangerous was happening and for $12.00 an hour, they didn't need to be blown to kingdom come at this lousy job. To add insult to injury, everything they brought into the building was searched by cops at the service entrance. Then each one of them was ordered to present themselves to have a photo ID made and to be fingerprinted. Four of them, who had previous records, declined to be fingerprinted and decided it was better to resign their positions than to go forward. They had been told that if they did not wish to submit, that no punitive action would be taken but that they could not work this show. What they weren't told is that as they were escorted toward the exit, each one of them would be diverted into an interrogation room where they would be exhaustively interviewed by federal agents. Each was asked to submit to a complete body search and each declined. By the time each one left the building, a federal agent had been dispatched to their residence to await their arrival.

      Particular attention was given to one gentleman by the name of Samuel Watkins, who had a previous conviction for child molestation. Although Watkins had led a blameless life for more than 15 years, his prior record and his unfortunate name put him under scrutiny. All the employees' lockers had been sealed off by the federal agents. Any possessions which were brought into the building were to be delivered to a cloakroom attendant who was a federal agent. There was a sign posted on the counter that anything left for checking would be examined and that by giving it into the checkroom, the owners consented to such an examination.

Before they left for the day, each one of these security employees of Harry Mills was cautioned that should they show up to work without their photo ID badge that they would be summarily discharged and/or arrested. Those badges were federal property and were to be returned to the federal officers upon demand. The one thing that the cops did not want was for some perpetrator to gain access by using a photo ID badge that belonged to one of these guys.

In his office, Mills spent a good part of the day telephoning, cajoling, begging and pleading with every temporary help agency and every security agency in the city to send him as many people as they could muster who could pass an exhaustive background investigation. Of course, all of these agencies knew what was going on from the newspaper reports and suddenly the net rates which they were demanding approached the same per hourly rate as one would pay for a state trooper to direct traffic. Harry was going to have to get an approval from Carly to pay these exorbitant rates.

The 6 o'clock news lead story was, "Threat Against the Vice President - - Real or a Hoax?" Not having any hard facts to go on, all of the TV pundits were very busy trying to cover both ends of the spectrum of possibilities. Nobody had heard from the mysterious Sam all day. Did that mean that the initial approach had been a hoax? Or had Sam been driven underground only to present an even greater danger once the show was open to the public? The story was worked to death by the electronic media. They had experts who would prognosticate on the amount of rainfall in the Sahara ten years from now and stopped just short of engaging Sister Marie the fortune teller to let the audience know what was going to happen next. They had excellent video library shots of previous Electronika shows from years past and plenty of footage of the locked doors of the Expo Center surrounded by guards and dogs. There were even the occasional shots of the public information officer from the ATF as he was smiling and trying to stay calm and unconcerned and basically saying he couldn't comment.

When Samantha left her apartment that evening, she drove about four blocks away to another hospital where she sought out the waiting room outside the surgical suite. Here she hooked up her fax machine again and dialed in to the number which Youngmann had provided to her. Samantha held the receiver to her ear and listened to the voice prompt which asked her to enter her personal identification number. She keyed in the number and listened to the message which instructed her to press 5 in order to send a fax. She pressed 5 and then pressed the start button on her fax. The transmission lasted only 18 seconds. As soon as she was done, Samantha disconnected, packed up and went on her way. In the

Operation Boomtown center, it was Janet McCauley who read the fax and called Brice Youngmann who was having dinner.

"Brice, we got a fax signal from your perp. Do you want me to read it to you?" Youngmann asked her to relay the message to him and she did. "How about $400,000 in 100's? I will call back in three hours for your answer. Put it on the machine. Sam."

At 8:00 at night he would have to call the Deputy Director and disturb him at his home to get authority to use $400,000 of the Bureau's money. It wasn't uncommon for them to advance funds in the case of kidnapings or terrorism activities and following the agency manual on procedures, he had to advise Mr. Atkinson of the ransom request. Technically, it wasn't exactly a ransom since no one had been kidnaped and it wasn't exactly a blackmail since no demand had been made. It was Darryl, who had suggested that a payment might be in order. All that Sam had done is ask how about a particular sum? One of the things he would have to do is get her to confirm in writing that he would accept the money in return for abandoning the attack on the show. He kept thinking in terms of "he".

The response from Washington was as swift as it was predictable. "Respond affirmatively to the suspect, stall for time." Several years earlier, Brice had been through a ransom situation where they had to get the president of a bank to authorize the opening of a vault at night. He didn't want to have to go through that again. Most of the major banks in town could put together $400,000 on short notice. But it was a considerable job to

144

have to make a record of all of the serial numbers and photocopy the bills with markings on them. The easiest way to do it would be to draw it down from the Fed where they would get bills in sequence. Sam hadn't said anything about the payoff being in old bills. This gave rise to some hope that maybe they could get away with using new notes which they could pick up in the morning from the Federal Reserve Bank.

The response from Albert Atkinson had been totally unpredictable and equally as swift. Atkinson had advised in no uncertain terms that $400,000 was being transferred to the First National Bank, Head Office, at 9 a.m., the next morning. It was being placed at the disposal of Mr. Brice Youngmann of the Federal Bureau of Investigation upon application and identification. Atkinson demanded that the payoff be made. In fact during the night before, he had been in contact with the home office of the overseas company which now controlled his firm. He had received three phone calls during the night from the Chairman of the Board, the President and the Executive Vice President of the holding company. The position of the company was that any arrangements should be made up to $2 million without hesitation. Beyond that sum, he was to request additional authorization. Hell, $400,000 represented a mere 20% of what his bosses thought they might have to pay off. With two days to show time and the Vice President due to show up, this was a bargain basement deal.

Three hours and five minutes after Sam had sent her fax inquiring about the $400,000 figure, she telephoned in again from the other side of town. She listened to the voice message which said to hear the current

145

outgoing message to press in her personal identification code. After she did so, she heard Youngmann say, "Sam, please believe me that this has been a difficult job for me as I know it has been for you. I have the authority to agree to pay you $400,000 if you will give me your written assurance that no attack of any sort will be initiated by you or anybody acting under your control, at your request or upon your instructions against the Electronika show now or at any time in the future. We will also need assurances that you are acting alone or that you have authority to speak for all other parties. If this is agreeable to you, you must give us something in writing that attests to your willingness to conclude the transaction. Once we receive that, we will go ahead and schedule the payments to be made in a manner to be mutually determined. Please send your message to me in a plain envelope addressed to Brice Youngmann at the Midtown Expo Center. You can have any taxicab or courier service deliver it with complete anonymity. We will not attempt to trace the delivery."

"Sure," thought Samantha. "It would be so easy to trace who gave an envelope to a taxi or to a delivery courier." Not to worry, Samantha had an idea. It was time to visit another one of her favorite libraries at the nearby university. It was a good thing that New York had so many wonderful institutions of higher education.

Samantha had a box of disposable surgical gloves which she had purchased in a drug store. When she went to the library, she sought out a study carrel in the back of the reference area where there were some old manual typewriters. Nobody used typewriters anymore since the computer chip had taken over the world. Samantha put on the latex gloves and withdrew a piece of plain white paper

146

from her briefcase which she inserted in the typewriter and quickly typed out the text which Agent Youngmann had requested. She then took an envelope which bore the insignia of a local hotel, folded the note into the envelope and carried it to a nearby water fountain where she tapped the gummed edge of the envelope into some of the moisture on the water fountain and caused it to be sealed. Thereupon, she returned the sealed envelope into her briefcase and removed her latex gloves.

Janet McCauley had come back from the airport with the tape which confirmed her suspicions. Now there was one Given. The suspect was a female or a short male who had used the women's lavatory at the airport. Human nature being what it is, they were inclined to rule out the possibility of a gentlemen using the ladies room. In a deserted airport concourse, a man would still automatically head for the room marked "Men."

The special "Sam" telephone rang. The recording equipment was activated and the agents in the room could hear the pips as somebody entered the personal identification code for the suspect known as Sam. No words were spoken. The suspect had activated the fax transmission and a fax was being received. The line went dead in less than a minute. The fax said only, "Youngmann, your letter is taped to the cement pier marked 3D in the Midtown Center garage. Sam."

"At last," thought Youngmann. "I got you now. Let me get my hands on that paper and my lab friends will have a field day." Youngmann ran from the building without his coat, and in less than five minutes had retrieved the letter which was taped exactly where Sam had indicated.   He quickly looked around the garage and determined that there were no surveillance cameras. Before leaving the garage, he questioned the lone attendant on the first floor of the garage who told him that nobody had entered or left the garage in the last 30 minutes. Terrific. The suspect had obviously used the pedestrian entrance, walked up three flights of stairs, taped the letter to the concrete pier and exited the same way he had entered without being observed.

When Youngmann got back to Operation Boomtown, he withdrew the envelope from the glassine cover into which he had placed the material retrieved from Sam.   With one end of the envelope in a tweezers, he gingerly sliced off about one-eighth of an inch of the opposing short end of the envelope and with a second pair of tweezers removed the note. The note was opened and flattened into a glassine document carrier and several photocopies were made both of the note and the envelope. The evidence was then carefully sealed and labeled by Agent Youngmann for identification.   It would be in Washington within a few hours. The last line that Sam had written in the note said that instructions for delivery of the money would be provided on the following day.

Youngmann took the call which came on the private line from Bill Wallace at ATF.   Wallace was steaming. "I understand you got a ransom request and you guys have decided to cave in for 400 G's.   Can you confirm?"

"Where did you get that from, Bill?" asked Youngmann.

"Well I got it from Bates at the newspaper who says that he got it by fax a few minutes ago from this guy Sam who just wanted him to know. You know, what the hell are we doing here? We're trying to conduct a covert operation in broad daylight and the suspect keeps giving all the Goddamn information to the newspapers. This thing is absolutely absurd."

Youngmann filled him in. "Look, the bottom line is that Atkinson has agreed to the 400 G payoff and, in fact, he insists on it. According to the bureau policy manual, we have to permit him to make the payoff. We can monitor it and we can apprehend afterwards but we cannot stop it. He's going to have the dough available tomorrow morning and I'm waiting for advice now as to how the subject wants the money."

Well for Christ's sake, we can't very well admit that in the press can we, Brice? That would make us look like a bunch of assholes. In fact, I'm beginning to think that we are looking like a bunch of assholes. I tell you what, I hope that when we do catch this joker, that I'm the one that takes him down because he's going down hard and permanently."

A team of more than 80 agents toiled through the night searching every bit of material that came into the exhibition halls. Dogs sniffed, agents with space-age looking probing devices probed, guards waited nervously, and the evening passed into the early morning daylight hours without incident. Another convoy of 18-wheelers would start arriving in a few hours to disgorge tons more of material.

The next message from Sam was sent to Brice's fax machine and a copy of it went to the newspaper. She loved the idea of putting the newspaper on the scent of the police so that nobody could hush up anything. Everybody was doing business in the open except for her.

The fax received from Sam was in verse. It said,

"Check the trucks, although it's folly.
Search the guests, won't it be jolly,
The show goes on, no matter what,
Let's hope the day ends without a shot.
For bombs or bullets are a "no go."
I prefer a subtler way to steal the show.
We'll see just how you boys can handle
The smoke and mayhem of my candle.
No bomb, no flame will mark the spot
Where reason ends and riots start
Tell the Veep hello for me
For I shall come there just to see
He's safe as in the Lord's great hands
Surrounded by protective bands.
No ATF, no Secret Service
Need attend nor get nervous . . .
No harm will come to our dear Veep.
But, the show will close.
My pledge I keep."

As soon as the fax had spewed out of the machine, Brice made several blowups of it and tacked them up on the wall and asked everybody to look at it. He

150

wanted to know what others thought of the note. The consensus was that they could rule out most of the former employees of Harry Mills' department. The fact that the writer was able to construct rhymed couplets indicated a level of education that transcended those of Harry's Heros. Janet pointed out that writer refers to "you boys" rather than you guys and felt that this was a female way of phrasing something. She felt it gave credence to her theory that the suspect was female. But how was she going to bring down the show without bombs and without bullets?

"We have every entrance to this area totally protected against any sort of explosive device or conventional weaponry. We've got x-ray machines set up, we have metal detectors, we have dogs." One of the other agents spoke, "Brice, what if this son of a bitch is planning to use gas? Remember the attack in the Tokyo subway system?"

Brice looked at him, "Yeah, how do we handle that?" "Well, it seems to me that there are some of those units that can determine chemical weapons as well as explosive weapons. I think we ought to get one or more of them over here tomorrow."

Brice shook his head a little bit and seemed to look at the tips of his shoes as he replied, "I can't do it. There are only a few of those units in the country and they are all assigned to critical airport use under TSA orders. There's just no way we can get our hands on them. So it's back to relying on body searches and conventional protective surveillance."

"Jesus Christ, you aren't suggesting that we

pat down 30,000 people a day coming into this friggin' show are you?" asked the younger agent.

Youngmann looked at him and for the benefit of everyone in the room said, "No, I realize that's impossible. I'm distributing a complete set of personality profiles to everybody who's going to be on perimeter control so that we will be on the lookout for particular types of people. As you know, this is the technique which has been used so successfully in airports for more than 20 years. The big problem is that we don't have profiles for terrorists that are quite as well documented as we have for dope smugglers. It seems that a lot of the terrorists, if they are successful, manage to blow themselves up along with their targets."

He continued, "And I don't know if you are aware of it or not; but Atkinson, the guy who runs this show, is insisting that he pay off 400 G's to this guy and we have to permit him to do it if that's what he wants to do. There's always a possibility that our guy will take the money and run.

Another agent spoke up, "Chief, you really believe that shit?"

Youngmann shook his head, "No, I don't. They usually take the money and still try to blow up the show or they don't come for the bait. But we just keep going, do everything we can and hope to God that we are right."

A report had come down from Washington in the meantime from the laboratory confirming what

Agent McCauley had suspected. It was entirely consistent with her theory that the suspect shown in the original tape recording had actually entered the ladies room and thereafter walked to the bank of telephones. The lab ended with a note saying that if there was any other evidence which it was desired they look at, to please let them know. Well, now they had some more evidence and in a matter of another hour or so, it would be on its way to Washington with a courier. They would pick off the fingerprints and start to run them on the computer. Hopefully, whoever it was had a record and it would show up in the NCIC or CODIS..

Brice left the control center and walked down the hall into the main lobby area of the Expo Center. He was just curious to see what was going on outside the building. As he walked through the lobby toward the glass doors facing the street, several bright klieg lights went on. Every television reporter's camera zeroed in on Brice Youngmann, special agent of the FBI. Through battery operated bullhorns, reporters yelled for Youngmann to come out and speak with them. He turned away immediately and retreated to his lair.

Monday was drawing to a close as Youngmann and his colleagues went over the material on the walls time and time again. It suddenly occurred to them that several of the communications had emanated from hospitals. Youngmann ordered a list of all hospitals and the facilities prepared and it turned out that there were more than 50 hospitals. He eliminated those Sam had already used and then marked off 12 more to which he dispatched a team of agents on surveillance mission.

They had determined that whoever sent the faxes had used a telephone extension somewhere in the hospital. But since these were all Centrex or PBX operations, the tracking equipment and caller ID would only provide the main number of the hospital facility and could not indicate which extension the call originated from. The anxiety and frustration levels were so high that Youngmann's people were quite prepared to order each one of these hospitals to close all entrances and exits except for the emergency room door and perhaps one other entrance. They would then lay in wait and should a trace come in indicating a particular hospital, then the agents would seal off the hospital completely and question every single person attempting to leave that hospital after the call. It was a shot in the dark but more than one case had been solved by this sort of approach.

There was no further contact from Samantha that night and the next morning she showed up for work on time having read the newspaper on her way into the office. Almost every facet of the previous days' activities had been accurately reported by the press. Samantha had made certain that they knew what was going on. The only thing they didn't reprint was her poem which she rather liked. Samantha was not aware that police would quite often withhold one or more pieces of evidence from publicly released stories which are known only by the perpetrator. It was with great coercion that the newspaper agreed not to reprint the poem. In fact, there had been no mention whatsoever of it.

Tuesday started off much the same as the day before. All of the work on the loading docks and in the exhibition halls continued at a snail's pace hampered by extreme security measures. All that the agents had come up with so far were half a dozen joints and a couple of methaqualones which were in the possession of the drivers. They confiscated the narcotics and promptly forgot about the drivers who they told to get the hell out and stay off the stuff. Not even the Drug Enforcement Agency would have been concerned over a few joints. In the great war on drugs if it didn't come to a half a ton, it wasn't worth prosecuting.

On an hourly basis throughout the day, the various agency chiefs checked in at the operation center. No word from Sam. What was he up to? What did he want? Where was he? What was happening? What would be next? And why the hell didn't he contact them?

Four hundred thousand dollars in old bills, mostly 100's, had been assembled at the First National Bank and were in a briefcase at any time that Mr. Brice Youngmann should require them. He had been provided a telephone number of a senior Vice President of the bank who would arrange for him to have access to the bank at any time day or night so that the money could be made available. Clearly, Atkinson was a man who could move mountains and he had done so.

There were about eight or ten agents in the operations room at the end of the afternoon and as they sat drinking their coffee and trying to figure out why they hadn't had any word from anyone. Janet McCauley spoke up, "I think she has a job!" All the eyes in the room turned and fixed upon Janet. "Say that again."

"I think she has a job."

It would fit. We have a female. She has a job. She's trying to lay low. She can't do anything during the day." One more little piece of the puzzle was now in place. They were looking for a 5'2" female who had a job. There can't be more than a million and a half of them around.

On Tuesday afternoon, the report from the lab was of no help. There were no prints whatsoever on the paper. They could confirm that the paper came from a block of paper which had been held at the top by a glued edge. It was a 20-pound white bond paper which was made by a particular firm and sold widely throughout the United States by every office supply and stationer in the country. Furthermore, they had determined that the reason there were no prints was that the person who wrote this note wore disposable latex surgical gloves. They found traces of a talcum powder of the type used on these gloves to keep them all from sticking to each other. Perhaps the perpetrator was employed in the medical field. It was just a guess. In fact, this particular product was also sold through every drugstore and supply shop in the country. They had carefully opened the envelope in a way to preserve the underside of the gummed flap and were not able to retrieve any prints from that area either. No DNA analysis would be attempted until and unless they had a suspect against whom a match might be sought. The envelope proved to offer no more than did the paper. Finally, the lab advised that the note had been typed on a Remington standard manual typewriter, for which they provided a model number. The ribbon appeared to be a fabric ribbon probably made by Carter. There was a slight abnormality in the letter M which would be used to provide a positive match should any of the field operatives recover the typewriter.

Once again, Janet's intuition seemed to be right on the money. She was thinking out loud. "I don't see this perp as working in the medical field. No doctor or hospital I've been to over the years has seen a manual typewriter since I was a little kid. They are all totally computerized. Even the friendly pharmacist at the local drugstore who used to hunt and peck to make up the little labels for the prescription bottles has those ground out automatically by a computer. Since the government started requiring that they keep an accurate data base of all the scripts that they fill for all of the patients, they all use an integrated software package. So that just doesn't make sense."

Youngmann asked, "Well, what about newspapers? Don't they have people there pounding typewriters?"

"Sorry boss, I think you must have been watching too many old movies. My guess is if you visit any newspaper around here, even some rinky dink weekly for shoppers, you're going to find that they are all totally computerized. I don't know who the heck would use a typewriter anymore." She continued, "But I'll guarantee you this. Sam doesn't own that typewriter. He or she, whoever the hell he or she is, is using equipment at various offices or institutions all over this town. We haven't got enough staff to try to go out and figure out where the hell this typewriter is. If it were up to me and I were the lead agent on this case, I wouldn't chase down that typewriter. I think it's a red herring."

From the reaction in the room, it was obvious that everyone agreed with Agent McCauley. "OK," said Youngmann. "Let's agree that we don't chase down the typewriter. We haven't got the time or resources for it. Where do we go from here?"

McCauley spoke again, "If I can offer a suggestion, Chief, I think where we ought to go from here is to an early dinner and maybe relax a little bit for a couple of hours. Take a look at the time frames of all of the contacts that we have had from Sam so far. Every one of the contacts has been either before 8 a.m., after 5 p.m. or on the weekends. Now we think that Sam is a female, we think she has a job which accounts for why we don't hear from her during the day, and I think my woman's intuition tells me it's going to be a busy night tonight."

At 4 p.m. Tuesday, a fight broke out on the loading dock when one truck driver who did not realize he was speaking with a federal agent, took umbrage at being unduly delayed in unloading his cargo. After he threw a roundhouse punch at the agent, he found himself lying on the concrete looking into the barrels of the drawn guns of four other agents who had been working on the loading dock. He had been taken into custody and was going to be conveyed to the local lockup. There he would be charged

158

with an assault on a federal officer. The incident information was telephoned upstairs to Brice who ran to the scene to speak with the officers involved.

When it was determined that none of the officers had initially identified themselves as federal agents, Youngmann took the officer involved aside, and asked just how anxious he was to press the very serious charge of assault on a federal officer. The younger officer sensing that his superior would prefer that this matter go away, decided that it was a misunderstanding. The belligerent truck driver could be released. One very lucky truck driver quickly left the marshaling area behind the Expo Center swearing never to take a job that brought him there again.

The Sam phone rang at 7:05 p.m. Every person in the room ran over to the machine to monitor the progress of the call. As before, the codes were entered to gain access and then to activate the fax receiver. Sam wanted to deal. The fax from Sam said, "O.K., on $400,000 in mixed old bills. You are to confirm within two hours that you have the money available packaged in a brown paper wrapper. You may confirm by written document which may be polled from your fax machine. A call will be placed in two hours to download your response. If all is in readiness, you will be provided the specifics on where and how to deliver the payment. You will be given enough time to get from your control center to the drop point plus five minutes. No deviation will be allowed.

Your movements will be monitored and observed."

Youngmann called his contact at the bank and relayed the instructions. The bank agreed that it would package the money as requested but required that Youngmann personally appear to sign for the money. Forty minutes later, one large brown paper package sat on the corner of Youngmann's desk containing $400,000 in U.S. currency. He wrote by hand a message which said, "Sam, the ransom you have required is in my possession and I am ready to deliver it. Please instruct me." This was playing very well into his hands because the money for the first time was being identified as a ransom and would require some delivery instruction coming back from Sam. So long as they caught him, this should be good for at least 20 years in the pokey. Blowups of all areas of metro New York were taped to the walls of the control center. On them were markers indicating the position of all resources, which included all agents assigned from various agencies and bureaus to Operation Boomtown, as well as command posts of local police and sheriffs.

At the front door of the Expo Center, Brice's car stood fully fueled. A technician had installed a high frequency radio transponder in his car which would allow a hovering helicopter or a fixed wing aircraft to plot the position of the vehicle at all times and coordinate other agents on the ground. A marked state patrol car was standing by to escort him as far as was practicable in the event that he had to traverse heavily traveled streets. When Sam's message finally arrived, it was very detailed.

"Mr. Youngmann, you are to drive your own car, alone. You are to have your flashing blue light on the front of your car on while you are driving so that your progress may be observed. You are to travel only by the roads indicated below. You are allowed five minutes to read this message and 60 minutes transit time to reach the drop point. When you leave the facility, you will use the marked roads to the interstate system and when you arrive at the barrier gate to the park, you are to park your car and you are to jog or run. I am assuming that you are fit and that a jogging speed of five and a half to six miles an hour would be no problem for you. You are to follow this map to the location of the drop and then turn around and exit the park by the same route. You are then to drive back to the Expo Center and await a phone call from me stating that I have retrieved your gift. Any attempt to put officers at the scene will cause this transaction to abort and all agreements between us shall be to no avail. I will stand by all aspects of my agreement and I expect you to do the same. Sam."

The agents scoured a map showing park which ran alongside the river not far from the interstate system to a major suburban thoroughfare less than 10 miles away. The park was laced with bike and hiking trails. The point that Sam had indicated for a drop was adjacent to a comfort station approximately three-quarters of a mile into the park. The park was closed after dark and would be deserted. The fact that Sam had not demanded that the agent come unarmed or stripped down to his jogging shorts suggested a face to face handoff wasn't contemplated. He would be carrying at least two weapons; one in his shoulder holster and his backup piece on his ankle. Although he had no great concern for his personal safety in this particular operation, he had to follow procedure. First he'd take care of his own personal safety and secondly, if he were going to attempt to apprehend the perpetrator, he would do so using whatever force was necessary. In this case, Youngmann had no thoughts about nabbing Sam with the money. He and his fellow agents would follow the money to see where it might lead them. If there were others involved with Sam, he would lead the agents to them. The process was simple. First; follow the money. Second; round up all the members and recover the money and weapons.

As Youngmann ran from the building, the state trooper assigned for escort came over to him.

"Just fall in behind me and if I get into trouble, you get in front of me and clear the way. We're going out to Epson Park. I got to enter from Thompson Drive. You drop off at the point where Thompson Drive swings in from Adams Road. While I'm in the park, you make yourself invisible near the exit and get a make on any vehicle or person leaving."

Youngmann was running ahead of schedule and pulled into the drive which led down to the park in 44 minutes. Only 58 minutes had elapsed by the time he had reached the drop point. He was sweating profusely and was short of breath. Youngmann placed the package in the middle of the track and called out repeatedly for Sam. He shone his flashlight around and saw nothing and heard nothing other than the rustling of small animals and the occasional bird taking flight at his intrusion.

Sixty-four minutes. Brice Youngmann turned and jogged back out of the park and with his blue lights flashing drove away from the scene. Unmarked cars driven by agents had cruised quietly into the area on the north side of the park and in the area where the park comes out to the highway. Other agents had been dispatched to the residential streets where the hiking and biking trails might permit someone to exit the park. Two devices had been planted in the money package. A short range FM transmitter which was designed to be found. But, the micro-chip transponder which had been buried in the package by Youngmann looked like a harmless wafer thin calculator. In fact, it would operate as one and it carried an advertising message for a company in Miami. Agent Paul Sykes was in a single engine Cessna 172 about two miles from the drop point. The screen in his cockpit was tuned to follow the transponder in the money package. He wouldn't bother to home-in on the FM transmission unless the micro transmitter signal failed. His radio crackled when Brice came on to say, "Bear 1 to Bear 2: Status."

Sykes replied, "Stationary, confirmed." The package hadn't moved. For more than 30 minutes, the plane made circles a couple of miles away from the drop in order not to have the drone of the engine constantly over the drop point. Thirty-five minutes after Youngmann had dropped the money, an agent crept out of the stand of trees near the drop zone and quickly shone a flashlight on the package. He doused his light and spoke into his microphone, "Weasel 4 to Bear 1. Object stationary, confirmed."

Sam wasn't coming to the baited package. She had watched the progress of Youngmann as he jogged down with his flashlight bouncing along and placed the package. She had listened to him as he called out her name. She had watched him jog off again. She had continued to play the waiting game against the possibility of a trap. When she saw the brief flash of light from Weasel 4, she knew that she had been right to bide her time. She lay motionless in the tall grass on the other side of the pond where she had observed the proceedings.

"So," thought Samantha. "They are going to leave the cheese in the mousetrap for awhile." She quietly made her way back to the roadway and walked the two blocks to where she had parked her car. No police were watching the road on the other side of the pond. In a few minutes she was casually driving through residential streets toward the interstate where she would meld into the traffic and go home. Tuesday was done. The negotiations had been held, the plan had been made, the trap had been set, but it would remain unsprung.

Samantha was pretty steamed. The more she thought about the money, the more she had come to a decision that she just as soon have the money as the satisfaction of taking down the show. But now she knew forever that she couldn't trust Youngmann or anyone else. She recalled the old joke, "I'm from the government and I want to help you." She composed several notes in her mind to Youngmann and Harry Mills as well as to the newspaper. She was playing fair and they weren't. She racked her brain as to how a handoff of the money might be effected with complete anonymity and security for her. She could think of no way.

No matter where the drop was made, it had to be retrieved and the danger was in the retrieval. In fact, the only one she could think of that ever really got away with a sizeable ransom was the guy who parachuted out of an airplane about 30 years ago over a national park somewhere in a western state. Neither he nor the money was ever seen again. "Well, screw it," thought Samantha. "If I can't have the money, at least I might be able to arrange that it does some good somewhere." She had formulated her plan and a little after midnight found herself again at a university library. She used the computer to print out a message which was then duly transmitted to Youngmann's control center. It said, "Youngmann, you are not to be trusted. That was a nasty trick that you boys tried to play tonight. On the other hand, I am trustworthy. I will still agree to the terms except the payments will not be made to me but to other beneficiaries. At 10 a.m. Wednesday morning you will call a press conference. Mr. Atkinson or anyone else acting for them will announce that the Electronika Internationale Exhibit Company is making four grants to local charities. He will present $100,000 <u>in cash</u> to each of the following four charities." The charities included a nondenominational shelter organization, the community chest, an organization which promoted equal treatment for gays and lesbians and an organization which operated shelters for battered women.

By the inclusion of the last two charities, there was no longer any doubt among any of the officers that they were dealing with a female perpetrator. Giving the money in cash to the charities did represent a tactical problem. If they gave away the money in cash, would the charities later agree to give it back? A donation made under duress might be revoked, later. However, he doubted that the Electronika guys would want to do that because of the negative publicity it would generate in the gay/lesbian and feminist movements. It would make them look like Scrooge at a Christmas party.

Youngmann ordered his troops to retrieve the currency and bring it back to the operation center and to send all of the watchers home. A team of agents was assigned to work through the night to contact the managers of the four charities at their homes, explain the situation to them, and get them to agree to appear for a televised news conference at 10 o'clock on Wednesday morning. Atkinson, in his suite of rooms at a nearby hotel, readily agreed and was grateful that it appeared to solve the problems of getting rid of this troublesome Sam.

It was less than 36 hours to show time and much remained to be done. Before Youngmann retired for the evening, the press had been contacted and all arrangements were made for the 10 a.m. show to go on.

❶❷

The reporters were assembled in the main lobby of the Expo Center by 9:30 a.m. Miles of cable were run from the cameras back to the remote trucks at the curbside and lights and reflectors were to be seen everywhere. The agents had cordoned off the rest of the building and refused to permit any of the employees to get near the press or for the press to enter the exhibition halls. This was to be a tightly controlled statement, not a news conference. At two minutes after ten, Albert Atkinson emerged from the operations room with four astounded representatives from the designated charities. They were not used to receiving donations in six figures and they had never received such a donation which was to be paid in cash. Atkinson read a prepared statement to the assembled media.

"My name is Albert Atkinson and I am the President of Electronika Exhibits, Incorporated. As you know, we have been an annual visitor to this wonderful community and we feel that New York is like a second home to us. Therefore, we should like to be good citizens of this community as well as the others in which we do business. It is with very great pleasure that I have with me today four ladies and gentlemen who represent charitable organizations in this community and to each of them we donate today the sum of $100,000. You will see in front of each one of these ladies and gentlemen a placard which bears their name and the name of their organization. In front of each one of them is a metal box which contains the donation. I will ask each of you now if you will be kind enough to open the box and display it for the ladies and gentlemen of the press."

On cue, the four grateful recipients each opened the metal cash box and tipped it up to display a solid mass of currency. One of the donees started to count the money. Atkinson laughed and turned to the cameras saying, "I can assure you, it is all there and if there is any shortage, we will make it up double the amount." Turning on his best public relations smile, he turned to the cameras again saying, "We open our greatest Electronika ever held in your fair city tomorrow morning at 10 a.m. at which time you may be aware we have the very great honor to be hosting a keynote address from none other than the Vice President of the United States. The exhibit halls will be open at 12 p.m. to all registrants. We want to thank the City and the management of the Expo Center for helping us to make this the most successful event ever in the history of trade shows. Thank you very much."

At this point, Atkinson turned to his left and exited the area. Dozens of questions were being shouted out from reporters which were being ignored completely by the agents and by Atkinson. It was the public information officer for the ATF who finally walked to the center in front of the table, turned to the assembled media and said, "We want to thank you all for coming and I believe that that concludes this press conference."

You can't fool the folks in the news business. They knew damn well that this wasn't a press conference, that this was a buy off and it was a publicity stunt. On the other hand, the story was still one that they had to run because nobody before had given away $400,000 in cash to charities including a couple of which were definitely second string operations. The story hit all of the television channels within a few minutes and the afternoon edition of The Ledger carried it front page in their evening edition..

Samantha was taking her lunch at her desk when one of her coworkers said, "Did you hear about the guy that gave away all the dough to some charities this morning? It was on all the news broadcasts." Samantha said that she hadn't and inquired what it was all about. Her associate proceeded to tell her that some guy who was a big shot with this trade show that's opening tomorrow had given away like $400,000 to four different charities, one of which operated shelters for battered women. Both of the women agreed that it was really a wonderful thing when an organization like that could think to help out such a worthy cause. Samantha really enjoyed her lunch and returned to work with a renewed sense of dedication. She would have to acknowledge Brice's good efforts today and get ready for tomorrow.

Back at the Expo Center, Red Casey was going through the motions of checking with Harry Mills over every detail of security for this show. The federal and state agents had determined that they would control the perimeter and respond in the exhibit halls in the event of an actual incident. But based upon the agreement that no incident would take place and the fact that the money had been paid at the insistence of Albert Atkinson, the agents had limited their participation in this matter. Casey, on the other hand, wasn't taking any chances. He ordered that every access way be controlled by one of Harry's men and he personally wanted to see and talk with the entire crew. He had been in touch with the federal and state authorities and they were making available a gas sniffer and a dog trained to sniff out explosives. By midnight tonight, the halls would be ordered cleared and sealed at which point the police search teams would enter the area and conduct a final search and walk-through.

Upstairs in the building, Bob Szymanski and his crew from the Secret Service were making all arrangements for the keynote address which would be delivered by the Vice President. The timetable called for his plane to touch down at approximately 9 a.m. He would travel by motorcade to the Expo Center and would arrive at 9:48 a.m. He would be taken to a secure holding suite in the facility and would appear on the stage at exactly 10:01 a.m. to deliver the keynote address. The standard security procedures for a speech by the Vice President had been put in place. All of the media people had been credentialed and checked. Each of the VIP's who would be in the actual hall where the Vice President was speaking had been credentialed. No service personnel would be allowed into the room while the Vice President was speaking.

Fortunately for the Secret Service, this room was designed to hold only 200-300 people in seminars. The speech was being televised on giant screens which had been placed outside the building and in the public areas of the Expo Center. Once the speech was concluded, the Vice President would be walked through the exhibit area by Atkinson and a select delegation of VIP's. He would enter the exhibit hall at 10:18 a.m. and conclude his walk through by 10:45. The plan called for him to exit the building at 10:50 and to be back aboard Air Force Two by 11:15 a.m. He would be at Andrews Air Force Base at 12:30 that afternoon.

Samantha worked a little later than usual since she had arranged for her personal day off on Thursday. She left the building at 6:15 and walked home the long way arriving at about 7 p.m. Dinner consisted of a Diet Coke and two more of those diet peanut butter bars that she had become addicted to. Her work for her employers finished; Samantha now set to work for herself. She drove over to another university library where she sought out more computers and printers and made up the last few messages that she would ever fax relating to this event. When she left the university, she started to head for a nearby hospital when a premonition occurred to her. She had to assume that they had traced all of her previous calls as coming from hospitals. It was time to pick another type of venue. The Metropolitan Transportation Authority, known as the MTA, had thoughtfully installed many coin phones in their subway stations throughout the community. Samantha went to the station behind the court house and paid the fare to enter the station. She went to the bank of coin telephones and connected up to Brice's fax equipment.

The fax took less than a minute to send and within a few seconds after that, she was out of the facility and back in her car. As the message was coming through the fax machine at the operation center, the agents had fixed the position of the call as coming from the MTA station. They could have no idea which side of the station the call was on. Considering the amount of traffic in the station, it was pointless to even dispatch an agent to the scene.

Youngmann was gratified by the tenor of the message although in his heart of hearts, he didn't believe a word of it. The message said, "Mr. Youngmann, thank you. You kept your word this time. As agreed, you may now relax and you have done a good job. Please tell Mr. Atkinson that I wish him all the best for the show."

Thursday morning. As Samantha was driving from her dental appointment to her OB/GYN, she tuned in one of the local talk stations which was proud to be carrying the address of the Vice President. The Vice President was a fine speaker who spoke eloquently about the inventiveness of American electronic engineering and our position as world leaders. He spoke of the competitiveness of American companies on the world stage and painted a glowing picture of our country continuing in the forefront as an economic superpower well into the next millennium. He carefully avoided mentioning the thousands of underpaid workers in the Indian subcontinent who were doing programming for these American companies or the assemblers in the Orient and Latin America who were putting together so many of these computers that were being bought by American homes and businesses. The speech was, if not inspiring, at least predictable and once he had paid his campaign promises by doing so, he made the obligatory tour of the exhibits and headed back to the inner sanctum of Air Force Two.

When the Vice President left the Expo Center, all of the Secret Service detail left within minutes and the agents from the Executive Protective Service were also called off the job. Now it was up to the paid security force, and Brice's people with the help of the ATF. Most of the agents had breathed a huge sigh of relief and had decided that the situation was now under control and that all was going to be just fine. The morning has passed without incident and it was now about 1:30 in the afternoon.

In one of the press rooms on the second floor, Suzanne Costello, Public Relations Manager for Electronika Internationale, was speaking with a group of reporters. She had prepared packets for each one of them with background information on the show and on the person of Albert A. Atkinson, originator and guru of this world class event. The "official" traffic count for the afternoon was determined by Suzanne from looking through the window which gave her a view over the exhibit floor. Based on her past observations, she estimated that some 35,000 people were in attendance in the facility at that very time. This would be the figure that would appear in the news articles and on all of the television reports. She had made certain that the press room was well supplied with coffee, beer, danish, fruit and sandwiches. A well-fed press was a happy press. There were also fax machines, teletype machines, and computers with modems available so that the reporters could file their stories instantaneously to any corner of the world.

Downstairs, one of the registrants picked up her badge and pinned it to her lapel and walked casually into the marshaling areas outside of the exhibit hall. She wasn't at all surprised to see that there were metal detectors in place and baggage scanners of the type used by airlines. The young woman placed her pocketbook on the scanning belt and walked through the metal detector. She smiled at the security guards as she retrieved her purse and slung it over her shoulder. Samantha headed down the long hallway to the last entrance point furthest away from where she had entered. She would start looking at the exhibits there and work her way back toward the main entrance. This was something she had normally done in any event because it allowed her to jump ahead of the crowd and work her way backwards. That way when she finished the exhibit floor and her feet were killing her, she would be back near where she had entered the building.

Samantha thought the exhibits quite interesting and genuinely enjoyed visiting these shows. Like any other visitor, she picked up the ubiquitous plastic bag and filled it up with as much literature and useless advertising novelties as she could. She latched on to some free samples of software which she thought would be fun to use and actually found a couple of programs which she could write a report on to her employer to show her diligence in watching out for their business.

At about 3:30 in the afternoon, Samantha had reached the middle hall of the exhibit area. The traffic here was probably at its most dense level. Along the back wall of the area were the bathrooms, concession stands and telephones. Samantha stood in line for a long while waiting to buy a cold drink and a hamburger with fries.

She sat at a small table near the stand while she finished her snack, then walked over to a nearby trash receptacle. She had on her tray three plastic baggies, which might have contained some health foods or other snacks. But, in this instance each contained the fruits of her lake-side experiments of the prior week. Samantha opened one corner of one baggie and tipped the baggie into the trash bin. She kept her tray with her to appear as if she were carrying something to a colleague in another area and sought out a second receptacle where she repeated her actions. Less than thirty seconds had passed from her first drop. Now she sought out a third receptacle closer to the center of the great exhibition hall, and made her final drop. This time she dumped in all the trash from her tray and placed the tray on top of the container. Elapsed time was one minute, 20 seconds. It was now about 3 minutes to show time. With an unhurried gait, she continued her inspection of the exhibits. By the time the trash receptacle started to emit dense smoke, she was some 40 feet away. An immediate alarm went off in the hall. One of the security guards who was simply doing what he had been instructed to do, noticed the smoke and went to the container. He saw no flame and fearing a bomb, he triggered the alarm by a call in from his walkie. Within a second or two, the public address system came on asking everyone to leave the hall in an orderly fashion and not to run. Of course, pandemonium broke out immediately.

Thousands of visitors started running, screaming for the doors. Shouts of fire, bombs, and other assorted perils were heard echoing through the hall, as the incendiary devices first produced a large volume of smoke followed by flames as the debris in the trash containers ignited.

It took almost 20 minutes to evacuate the hall. Many exhibitors refused to leave and many of the attendees similarly stood their ground. Police with drawn guns were everywhere and a bomb disposal team in heavy padding and face masks approached this evil-looking trash receptacle in the center of the hall. Within 30 minutes it was all over. The trash receptacle and its contents had been removed but the Electronika show was effectively over for that day. The media people in a press room overlooking the exhibit hall were able to observe and photograph the mayhem below. The heat generated from the fires in the three cans had created havoc just from burning the trash in those containers but, nothing had blown up.

The dogs which were brought in to sniff around responded as if nothing explosive were at hand. The ATF people were stumped. This was not an usual explosive device; it was at the worst a smoke bomb. Based upon the lingering scent and some further analysis, the ATF technician advised the other agency people that his best guesstimate was that this was a diversionary smoke screen that was created by exposing white phosphorus to the atmosphere. It couldn't have been prevented because none of the detection devices would have picked up the introduction of the phosphorus into the facility.

❶ ❸

4:30 p.m. The fax was received at Youngmann's control center and a copy was also sent to the press. "Mr. Youngmann, while I agree that you did do the honorable thing this morning by handing out the money, you must agree that you were very sneaky and untrustworthy the day before. Accordingly, it was necessary that you have a small punishment. You now know that I can stop this show at any time. It is obvious that I can pass through your security devices and perimeter control with ease. I require from you one additional sign of your rehabilitation and good faith. All electronic screening devices including the x-ray conveyor belts and the metal detectors are to be removed before the show opens tomorrow morning. If I find that any of them are still there when I come to attend, then I reserve the right to close the show down. Please do as you are told. Sam."

At an emergency meeting that night attended by Albert Atkinson, Red Casey, Harry Mills, Carly Bentwood and representatives of all of the police agencies involved, the dilemma was discussed. Do they remove the perimeter control devices or not? Atkinson argued that since they had proved to be totally useless and had done nothing but inhibit people from attending his show, that they served no purpose to stay in place. Youngmann knew better and his professional judgment said to keep them in place, however, he had no choice but to yield to the demands of Atkinson and Bentwood since this was a show being conducted on private property.

By 2 a.m. all of the perimeter control devices had been removed and by 4 a.m., 14 more closed-circuit television cameras had been installed, all wired to Operation Boomtown control center. By 10 a.m. the next morning, 58 police agents were in the facility dressed in plain clothes. Each one of them was wired with a subminiature microphone and transmitter and the exhibit area had been divided into sectors. Like policemen patrolling a beat in a city, each one of these individuals had a particular sector to patrol. Realizing that they were up against somebody who was chary, they took the added precaution of putting together a play schedule that rotated each agent from one sector into an adjoining sector every 15 minutes. If the suspect were watching the watchers, she wouldn't see anything unusual.

The exhibit hall opened at 10 a.m. on Friday. Samantha had written up an interesting report for her boss featuring some of the software which she had seen at the show on Thursday and presented it to him during the coffee break. He was suitably impressed and asked her some questions about its capabilities. He played right into her hand. She explained that with the mob that was at the show, she was unable to frame all the questions and get all of the answers that were necessary but would be glad to brave the crowds again if her boss wanted her to go back there this afternoon. It seemed like a good idea to him since he'd rather that she put up with that mob scene than that he go there. By 12:30, Samantha was through work for the day, had wolfed down her lunch, and was at liberty to return to the Electronika exhibit.

178

Franklin Hobson had served his country in the armed forces. In the course of doing so, he had contracted one or more diseases from which he never recovered. In fact, he was a drug addict and there was no chance that he was ever going to be anything else. Anything that looked like a chemical or natural psychedelic substance that he could swallow, inhale, inject or otherwise utilize was all fair game to him. Franklin existed on odd jobs which he picked up from time to time as a security guard or working unloading trucks or the occasional light construction job. On this day, he was working at one of the concession areas cleaning up after the customers. As a keen observer of human nature, he noted the pickpocket who was rifling the purse of a woman customer while she was waiting for her order at the stand. He followed the man to the men's room where he quietly brought to the other gentleman's attention the anti-social nature of the act which he had observed. The first gentleman had relieved this young woman of a wallet, a gold pen, and a bottle of some kind of pills or other chemical substance.

A brief discussion ensued during which time Franklin suggested that his obligation was to call for the police and to have this gentleman arrested. After all, there had been a bomb scare and everybody was very nervous about shenanigans going on. The pick-pocket begged and pleaded that he really wasn't a career criminal and that he was homeless and hadn't eaten in four days and he really didn't intend to keep everything that he took from the woman and, as they discussed it further, it was agreed that this hapless urban outdoorsman would retain the cash from

179

the wallet, and return to Franklin the woman's pills and her wallet with her credit cards and ID. Franklin could be a hero and simply say that he found the wallet tossed into the trash bin in the gent's room. This wasn't an uncommon occurrence in events such as this show.

Franklin left the men's room and headed off to the lost and found with the wallet. On the way, he found a uniformed officer and decided to turn in the property to him along with his own name and phone number as the finder. If there were a reward forthcoming, it would be much to his credit and would be passed on to him. A short time later, Franklin lay dead of phosphoric poisoning in the emergency room of Mercy Hospital.

Samantha followed her plan until she reached the area where she expected to set off the additional reaction devices. When she went to her purse for more baggies she was panic-stricken to find that the brown bottle was missing. At first she thought perhaps she had dropped it somewhere but remembered that she had not been into her purse once she had entered the hall. If she had lost it, she lost it before she got there. When she discovered that her wallet was missing as well, she realized that she had been the victim of a pickpocket. Samantha had placed a few dollars in the pocket of her skirt which she used to pay for her purchases at the concession stand. Somewhere in the jostling crowd, somebody had opened the flap of her purse and removed several items. She knew nothing about the death throes of her would-be benefactor.

But, what to do about the missing billfold? It was probably long gone. She would have to call her various credit card companies to cancel her accounts and have new numbers assigned and she would have to go through the aggravation of getting a duplicate driver's license issued. Samantha was really angry with herself for having been victimized. She was supposed to be the predator, not the prey.

There were the usual number of incidents in the exhibition hall on Friday. The security people had called in the police officers to arrest three hookers who were working the crowd, and one pickpocket who they caught red handed trying to lift a wallet from an undercover policeman. Two other visitors were drunk and started a fight and both became the guests of the county for a few hours while they sobered up. Lost and found reported four briefcases turned in, one electronic pocket secretary, one audio cassette recorder, and various items of personal clothing. These were all duly logged in and placed in the lost and found locker of the Expo Center.

Franklin had turned in the wallet to the first uniformed officer with whom he came in contact. It happened to be a State Trooper who was working on a special assignment for the Expo Center. He did not know the normal routine and turned over the wallet to one of the FBI agents. About 4 o'clock in the afternoon, the woman who took care of lost and found inquiries called Harry Mills on his walkie to ask if he knew anything about a wallet belonging to a Samantha Harrison. The woman was down at the lost and found desk and hopping mad. She was screaming that it was the responsibility of the Expo Center to make it safe for the guests and what the hell kind of operation were they running anyhow? Bomb threats, death threats and smoke bombs and now pickpockets. It was too much to bear. Harry asked his employee if the woman who was so agitated could overhear his response. When he got a reply in the negative, Harry simply told the clerk that he would make inquiries but in the meantime just get rid of her. Take her name and address, quiet her down and get her out. Harry's feet were killing him and he needed a quiet and almost sane place to hide for a few minutes. He dropped in at the Operation Boomtown control center to pick up a cup of coffee and put his feet up in the company of his professional colleagues.

Harry poured himself a cup and slumped into the closest padded chair. The agents there were swapping war stories about their past victories and loves and defeats and the events of the day. When the time came for Harry to offer his comments, he said how this was just a typical day of dealing with tens of thousands of tourists in a major event such as this.

"You know," said Harry, "it runs the gamut from some employee who ate something that he shouldn't have and croaked of food poisoning to some broad who got her wallet boosted and is pissing and moaning at us like we did the heist."

One of the agents was able to clue Harry in that the gentlemen who died wasn't the victim of food poisoning but had ingested phosphorus, the same stuff which was used to set off the smoke bomb in the previous day's escapade. A team of agents had been dispatched immediately to his last known address and a thorough search had been made. They ripped apart his living space completely and found absolutely no evidence of anything that would link him to the mysterious Sam. "Anyhow," continued the agent, "one of the state troopers brought in this wallet about an hour ago. You might want to take a look at it because it could be the one that your customer is looking for. I was going to bring it to your office at the end of my shift but I can't leave here while I'm monitoring the equipment."

Harry opened the wallet and pulled out the driver's license. There was the picture of Samantha Harrison. "Son of a bitch. Yep, that's the broad, her name is Samantha Harrison."

"What did you say her name was?" screamed Agent McCauley.

"Samantha Harrison," said Chief Harry Mills.

"Oh yeah, well don't be in such a hurry to give that wallet back. Lemme take a look at it." The agent emptied out the contents of the wallet on the desk. It contained an American Express card, a regular Visa card, charge cards from five different stores and several photographs of young people who were presumed to be relatives. There was no money in the wallet. What did intrigue Agent McCauley was a business card from a local restaurant which had inscribed on the back of it some figures. They were "R335.83." McCauley reached for her walkie and quietly asked all of the agents on duty to keep an eye out for Samantha Harrison. She passed the description of the woman to them and told them that if they encountered her, that they were to politely ask if she was Samantha Harrison and if so, tell her that her wallet had been found and please conduct her to an interview area. They were not to bring her to the operations room.

Samantha was just leaving the building in the midst of seven or eight other people. A well-dressed man in his mid-30's asked if she were Ms. Harrison. At first, she was startled particularly when she noticed the coiled wire leading up to the earpiece which he was wearing. He was obviously a security person. Her brain raced ahead. They must have found her wallet and looked at her description and broadcast it to these people. Samantha turned and quietly said, "Yes," as she flashed a smile at the police officer. "Do I know you?"

"No, Ma'am, I'm with the security detail here but I just received a broadcast of a description such as yours. Did you misplace a wallet here at the show?"

"Well, I wouldn't say misplaced it. Actually, it was stolen from me somewhere in the show. Do you have it?"

"Yes, Ma'am, it's being held for you. I will be glad to take you to the person that has custody of your property." It was interesting the way he used the phrase "custody of your property" as opposed to holding onto your wallet.

Samantha was met in a small interview room by Special Agent Janet McCauley who was carrying her wallet.

"Are you Ms. Harrison?"

184

"Yes, Ma'am, I am," replied Samantha.

"Well I'd ask you for some ID, but I've already seen the ID in your wallet and I guess you are who you say you are. Would you please inspect your property and let me know if anything is missing."

Samantha went through her wallet quickly and answered that the only thing that appeared to be missing was about $80 in currency. "I don't suppose somebody in your office found that, too?"

"No, Ma'am, there was no money in the wallet when it was turned in to us. The wallet was recovered from a trash bin in the mens room."

Samantha looked at the agent, "Well, I guess it's not so bad. At least I don't have to cancel all my credit cards."

"Was there anything else missing from your purse at all?" asked the agent.

"What was she getting at?" thought Samantha. Did she know about the phosphorus baggies? No, that was too far fetched to be true. It just couldn't be. Samantha pretended to search through her purse and while she was doing so, the agent said, "Look, why don't you just do it the easy way. Empty it out here and you can then spread it out and make sure that nothing is missing." Instinctively, Samantha did as the agent suggested. She removed her compact, various cosmetic items, her wallet, two rings of keys, a pad of paper, two pens and a few other bits and pieces normally found in ladies' purses. McCauley's eyes were fixed upon the pad of paper. It was a five by eight pad of the same size as the note which had been received two days earlier by Youngmann. It was bound with glue at the top.

"Careful," thought McCauley, "we don't want to put her on guard." McCauley spoke to Samantha. "Ms. Harrison, just routine but I need to make sure I write down your name and address. I forget because we were in such a hurry to get this wallet back to you. Can I just borrow a piece of that paper and I'll write it on there." Without waiting for an answer she reached for the pad and ripped off the top piece of paper. As Samantha provided her name and home address and telephone number to the agent, she wrote them in small hand at the bottom edge of the paper which she then laid to one side. Looking at Samantha she said, "Well, I guess there is nothing more I can do for you. If there is anything you need at any time, just get in touch with one of the security people here at the Center."

Samantha put her property back in her purse and departed the interview room, leaving the building by the most direct route. She hadn't noticed that one business card which had been in her wallet when she lost it wasn't there when she recovered it.

As soon as Samantha had left, McCauley returned to the operations room where she picked up a glassine evidence envelope and returned to the interview area inserting the piece of paper into the envelope. To her somewhat trained eye, it could have been from the same block of paper. She radioed for Youngmann to please return to the control center.

186

"Brice, you can call it woman's intuition or serendipity or whatever you want to call it, but I got a funny feeling about this woman. Let's go over something. We know that Sam could be female. We know that the person is about 5'2". This woman, Samantha Harrison, is 5'3" according to her driver's license. I eyeballed her when I gave back her wallet. She could be that shadowy form that we got on the tape from the airport. She had nothing unusual in her purse and she didn't behave in any way that was suspicious at all. She was kind of annoyed about the money being lost, but that's typical when somebody boosts a wallet; they strip out what they can use and then throw away the rest. But, she did have a pad of paper in her purse that could be the same type as the pad from which the paper came on the note written to you. I managed to get the top piece of paper off the pad and I'd like to have it shipped up to the lab for a positive ID on it tonight."

Brice was beginning to have tremendous respect for McCauley. Whether it was intuition, serendipity or just the application of raw intellect, he had to admit that she was the only one that seemed to be getting anywhere at all on this case. "OK, I'll have it sent up there but let's follow the thread. Assume for the sake of argument that it's the same paper as the paper that was used in the note to me. There must be millions of those pads out there. And assume for sake of argument that it's got some fingerprints on it. We know it was in her purse so why shouldn't it have her fingerprints?"

"Right, Chief," said McCauley. I wouldn't waste time testing it for prints. Ask the lab to test it for talcum."

187

Brice Youngmann sat back in his chair, smiled at McCauley saying, "God, you are a bright one, aren't you?" Youngmann continued, "OK, we got nothing to go on other than your intuition and this piece of paper but let's just play it cool. We will keep security at the present level here at the hall for now." He called an agent in to take this piece of evidence and to dispatch it on a priority basis to the lab in Washington. He wanted the lab to work on it tonight and told them to get whatever authorizations were necessary for the overtime. He needed the answers as quickly as possible. Next, Youngmann called in a team of agents and ordered them to set up on the home address of Samantha Harrison. He was able to give them a photo blowup of her driving license which they used for ID. McCauley was the type who thought of everything. She had quickly run it through the copier before returning the materials to Harrison.

Samantha didn't return directly home. She had parked her car in a garage near work because she knew she had some errands to do at the end of the day. When she came to work in the morning, she didn't know that she would be back at the show that afternoon. She went to the MTA station and walked to where she had left her car. Then, Samantha drove to the office supply store and returned the fax machine. In fact, it was a fortuitous situation because the clerk returned to her $236.97 which replenished the money that she had lost in the theft. When she got to a strip center with a supermarket in it, she pulled around the service road behind the strip center and casually tossed the acoustic coupler up into the dumpster. About

188

eight miles away, she drove behind another shopping center and got rid of the pad of paper. It had occurred to her that the note to Youngmann had been typed on a piece of paper from that pad. When Samantha returned home about 9 o'clock that night, she didn't notice two cars of agents; one at either end of her block who were surveilling her. Nor, after she had entered her apartment, was she able to see the agent who placed a radio transmitter behind the bumper of her car.

Across the street from her stood a step van from a company which did steam cleaning of rugs. She couldn't see nor know that a video camera with a very fast and long lens was trained on her from that van. Inside the van, recorders picked up anything said on her telephone lines. Ultra sensitive parabolic microphones were trained on the windows of her home to pick up conversation within. All they picked up was the sound of her television. Apparently, she lived alone, and she neither received nor made any phone calls that evening. About 11:30, the light in her living room went off and the light in her bedroom went on. About 15 minutes later, that light went off. Samantha Harrison had gone to sleep.

❶❹

There would be little sleep for Janet McCauley that night. Using the copier machine, she had enlarged the back of the business card until the writing stood about four inches high on a piece of paper. She had it propped in front of her. What did this stand for? This was a conundrum that stumped even the redoubtable Janet. She made an additional copy of the cryptic note and enclosed it with the exemplar of paper which was being sent to the lab. She caustically wrote at the bottom of it, "Have any of you nerds got any idea what the heck this stands for? Please advise."

3 a.m. McCauley's telephone had been ringing incessantly and it finally roused her from a deep sleep. It was Youngmann. "Janet, you ought to change your name to Sherlock Holmes. The paper you sent to Washington has talcum on it. The same type and the same grit as on the note which we got from Sam. I told the guys on the street to stay put and we're going to go in to take her at 4 a.m. The local guys want time to get the press there so that they can have some favorable coverage of the bust."

Janet flew out of bed and was dressed and out of her apartment in less than five minutes. At 4 a.m., a phalanx of agents spearheaded by Brice Youngmann and Janet McCauley came careening into the street where the suspected terrorist, Samantha Harrison, a/k/a Sam, lived a quiet life.

The red and blue lights woke up many of the residents and these were augmented by the glare of dozens of television camera crews who were there to record the scene for posterity. Agents swarmed over the building and blocked front and rear exits while they shined high intensity lights on all windows and walls on the exterior of the building. Four agents, including Youngmann and McCauley, rushed up the stairs and put their shoulders to the door to Samantha's flat which gave way easily under their impact.

As the officers flooded into the small rooms of Samantha's apartment, they were poised with drawn guns gripped in two hands in the controlled firing position. There was no response to the command, "Police - - drop your guns, get on the floor!" The TV in the living room was still on, although the station to which it had been tuned was now off the air. The pass-through from the kitchen to the dining area held the remains of some Chinese food and an empty bottle of Bordeaux. The door to the bedroom was open. Samantha lay sprawled on the bed. She was still dressed in her clothes. The telephone had been left off the hook and a bottle of Valium stood on the night stand next to her alarm clock.

Samantha awoke and shook her head as if to toss off the shrouds induced by the drug and the wine. "What the hell . . ." Before she could finish the sentence, she was pinned down by one agent who threw himself across her chest while he grabbed for her right wrist. A second cop had taken hold of her left wrist and yet a third one was now holding her ankles firm in some kind of wrestler's grip. They pulled her forward and cuffed her hands fast behind her back. Janet was searching under the pillows and bed clothes for a weapon, while another agent pulled Samantha from the bed and stood her against the wall, where he held her by pressure to her chest.

Janet finished the search of the top of the bed, and under the bed. As she got up, she said "Clean."

"OK, Samantha." said Youngmann, "It's all over, let's go."

"What the hell are you talking about?" Samantha had regained her composure, now. "I haven't done anything - and I don't know what the fuck you're talking about." She was screaming now and trying to twist out of the grip of the agents who held her tightly by her elbows.

Youngmann looked at Janet, "You want to do the honors?"

Janet McCauley stood in front of Samantha Harrison. "Samantha Harrison, you are under arrest for the bombing of the Electronika show and for the unlawful possession of explosive devices. You have a right to remain silent. You have the right to consult a lawyer . . . ."

"You're damn right I have a right to a lawyer. And I want to call him right now."

"You can make a call after you've been processed." It was Brice Youngmann who had interrupted. He pulled Samantha by the arm. "Let's go." Youngmann,

192

McCauley and one other agent pushed and pulled Samantha out of her apartment and stuffed her into the back seat of their car. They ignored the crowd which had gathered to watch the drama unfold. But, before they shoved Samantha into the car Youngmann brought the group to a halt long enough for the media horde to get their pictures. He made no statement. The only statement the media got was Samantha screaming something about "Police assholes" which would be bleeped out of all the broadcasts.

They had 72 hours to hold Samantha before the law required that she be brought before a Magistrate. Plenty of time to complete the case work. Samantha was less than cooperative when she was turned over to the Marshal Service. They would hold her in an isolation area downtown pending further instructions. She refused to give any information other than her name. She made it as difficult as possible for the cops to print her and photograph her. There was no matron on duty during the night, so Samantha was placed in holding tank by herself. She would be strip searched as soon as a female agent or matron were available. She was furious, and remained so during her confinement.

It was eight the next morning before a matron was brought to the holding pen. Samantha was clean. She was permitted to make a phone call at 8:17 a.m. It was to Ed Garville, one of the country's most respected criminal trial lawyers, whose home was in Stamford. When the agents recording the call were convinced that it really was Garville to whom Samantha was speaking, they obligingly stopped their tape. Deliberate monitoring of an attorney-client conversation was a real no-no. Especially when it was a lawyer like Garville who would serve you up your own entrails for breakfast.

By nine o'clock, Harry was playing host to a dozen or more reporters and camera crews in front of the Expo Center.   He detailed for them the massive investigation which he, Harry, had organized and supervised.   Harry described how he had slept at the Center since the crisis began, and left no stones unturned to ferret out this dangerous villain.   Harry had often been found sleeping at the Center even when there were no crises to attend to. But, this was different. This was the lime light.   He was a celebrity, and he was loving it. Certainly he would be getting a call from Phil or Oprah by the end of the day.

Youngmann wasn't happy at the ten a.m. staff meeting.   The sweep of Samantha's digs had produced nothing.   No chemicals other than artificial sweeteners and creamers, and they had even analyzed those to make certain.   No bombs, fuses, plans, books, notes. Nothing. Zero. Bupkis.   They had pulled everything from every drawer and cabinet.   Agents checked the undersides of the drawers for envelopes which may be taped up there, and unfastened the kitchen cabinets from the walls.   They checked the water tank in the bathroom, cut into every cushion and pillow, pulled off the back of the TV to see what might be cached inside.   They flipped through every book and magazine.

While one crew was turning Samantha's apartment into something that looked like a direct hit in Kabul, a second was searching through the trash in the barrels behind the apartment and pulling apart the storage area, much to the discomfort of the other tenants whose property was being handled as rudely as Samantha's. Two more agents were busy interviewing all of Samantha's neighbors. Net result from these teams. Nada.

The search did turn up a photograph of her father which was taken out of a silver frame on her bureau. When the photo was removed, a newspaper clipping was found folded behind it. The yellowed item was an obit about Paul Harrison who left a widow and daughter. The family had requested no flowers. Gifts could be sent to a vocational training center for senior citizens. It was nothing out of the ordinary and certainly didn't tie her to the attack on Electronika.

Brice was exasperated. "I think she damn well did it. Whadda you think?" The agents in the briefing room were less certain then Youngmann. Janet spoke up, "I'm damn sure she did it, boss. I just don't see how we're going to prove it right now."

Youngmann tossed her a folder. "Well here's the rest of the news. We got two kinds of news, boys and girls. Bad news and worse news. This is a summary of all the physical evidence so far. No prints on the note to me from the garage. No evidence of anything in her apartment or her car. We turned over her workplace and that rang up a big zero, too. There's one chance only and that's a DNA match from her to the gummed back of the envelope, and you can bet your next pay raise that we

195

aren't gonna get a blood sample from this lady unless she cuts herself in the cell. And for the real bad news, she's hired Garville. The circus is coming to town."

Youngmann's prophecy was based on past experience. By noon, Ed Garville was being shown on every mid-day news broadcast. "The police have arrested a totally innocent person. I have no idea of who is responsible for the attack on the show; but I can assure you that it was not Samantha Harrison. That's all I can say at this time. Ms. Harrison will be released by tonight and we will have a statement for you tomorrow. Thank you."

Garville looked good. Behind that Good-Ole-Boy facade there was one of the sharpest minds in the business. The only thing that didn't add up was Garville representing Samantha. He usually worked for the big money crowd; the dopers, swindlers and celebrities among the criminal elite. He billed out at $1500 an hour and it was said he must pull down more than two million a year.

The Assistant United States Attorney was bright enough. He had been practicing for 12 years, and had a distinguished law school record. His scorecard of convictions was impressive. He was batting 94% for all cases he prosecuted. But he had tried five cases against Ed Garville and his batting record against Garville was a depressing Zero. Garville had requested and been granted an emergency hearing at 3 p.m. that afternoon. Actually, the Magistrate had indicated he would be amenable to hear the motions right after the lunch break. But, while Garville's assistants were grinding out the pleadings and copies of supporting case law, his communications director was busy making sure that the hearing chamber would be packed with reporters.   Garville never shied away from publicity.

The Courtroom was packed.   After the Magistrate had been seated and read through the motions stacked on his desk, he asked the attorney for the government what cause they had, if any, to continue to hold Ms. Harrison.   It didn't take long.   Assistant U. S. Attorney Moorefield stated the case for the government and pointed out that he was quite certain a DNA match would prove conclusively that nobody other than Samantha could have done the deed.

"Well, we got a problem here, Mr. Moorefield." said Judge Riley.   "You see, I have your motion for a blood sample, and I have Mr. Garville's opposition to it. And, I have to tell you, I think he's right on this one.   If you have nothing at all to support an arrest or her continued detention, then it would compound a grievous error to compel this defendant to submit to a blood test.   You know the law.   It goes directly to unreasonable search and seizure."   Moorefield was standing quietly by the side of the counsel table.

Judge Riley continued, "So unless you have something else, some relative evidence, any evidence at all, and compelling reason to continue this woman in custody, then I have no choice but to grant Mr. Garville's motions and order her release, *instanter*."

Moorefield was staring at his shoes and raised his hands, palm upwards in supplication   "There's a compelling public interest in preventing this defendant from unleashing another attack, Your Honor.   We can

197

prove her involvement with the DNA . . ."

He never got to finish his sentence. "The motion of the government for a blood test is denied. The defendant is released without condition." The edict was punctuated by the gavel slamming on the wooden block in front of Judge Riley.

The circus had come to town all right. Garville marched his client out of the Court House and into the limousine which stood at the curb. As the limo pulled away from the curb, Ed Garville and Samantha Harrison hugged each other tightly in a winner's embrace. That evening, Samantha dined with Garville at his club. She listened carefully as he explained what a blood test might lead to. Garville never asked her if she did it. She answered all of his questions and signed the contract which Garville had brought with him. Her bills for his representation would be credited against the royalties on her contract which granted to Garville the exclusive rights to her story.

In the aftermath of the embarrassing arrest Brice Youngmann and the rest of the police were nowhere to be found. It was just Harry Mills, who seemed to be oblivious to the debacle, who was basking in the glare of the reporter's lights. The invitation never came from Oprah, but he did get 4 minutes on a locally produced late night show. Harry's line, to which he stuck, was "I know who pulled this job and I stopped her. What more proof do you need than the fact that this Center is still standing?" He finished every interview with his sign-off, "The Show *Will* Go On." None of the stories released to the press mentioned anything about somebody named Franklin who had died of phosphoric poisoning, or of a pickpocket who had been the catalyst in breaking this case. Life went on pretty much as it had before, and the attack on Electronika quickly became yesterday's news

Special Agent in Charge, Brice Youngmann, received a letter of commendation from the Director which was placed in his permanent personnel file. He was transferred to Houston a year later.

Harry Mills gratefully accepted a check from Albert Atkinson in the sum of $50,000 as a small token of the esteem in which he was held and as a way of saying thank you for a superlative job well done. Harry immediately told Carly to take the job and shove it. He took Mary to dinner at the Ritz that evening. The next day he bought a huge new flat screen TV, and after a brief vacation, accepted a job as chief of security at a major hotel. When the deal was made to make a TV movie based on the bombing of the Electronika show, Harry joyfully signed on as a consultant as arranged by Ed Garville. Harry thought the show was the best he had ever seen.

Agent Janet McCauley received an open letter of commendation from the Director plus three additional days of paid leave. She was subsequently promoted to the rank of Inspector and named as the Law Enforcement Liaison Officer attached to the Embassy in Moscow. She had gotten up in the agency - - but was consigned to a thankless task in Putin's wild west. She never did get to see a note that got tossed out with the lab report. "We nerds are happy to advise that the inscription you sent us is a Dewey Decimal System reference code. We took the liberty of checking it out and for your information, it is the catalog code for the *Anarchist's Cookbook*. It's a lovely piece of reading. Enjoy!"

Several weeks later, a library intern working at the Library found that a drive on one of the public access computers had somehow been partitioned. It was just cutting into the storage space that should have been available. There was nothing intelligible on that drive and with a few keystrokes he wiped out all of Samantha's files and restored the drive to its original configuration.

After her arrest, Samantha was fired from her job. Garville loaned her $20,000 to get herself resettled in Seattle where she works for FEMA. The studio paid $425,000 for the rights to Samantha's story, of which she received $195,000 after Garville's fees were deducted. It was a good day's work all around.

Sean "Red" Casey was still Director of Security for Electronika Internationale when a large bomb exploded in the exhibition hall of one of their other shows, a few months later. He died soon thereafter..

-0-

Fact or Fiction ?

September 11, 2001:   The worst act of terrorism ever visited upon the United States.   The World Trade Center towers are destroyed and thousands died.   America becomes incredibly security conscious.

September 15, 2003: The American Society for Industrial Security (ASIS) holds its huge international trade show at the Morial Convention Center in New Orleans. The author picks up entry credentials without having to provide any identification.

After leaving the exposition hall he drives to the allegedly secured loading docks at the back of the building, along the river's edge, and enters through an unguarded freight entrance. Good thing Samantha didn't know about it.

LaVergne, TN USA
22 August 2009
155538LV00004B/30/P